Asleep

Banana Yoshimoto was born in 1964. She is the author of
Kitchen, *N.P.*, *Lizard* and *Amrita*. Her stories, novels and essays
have won numerous prizes both in Japan and abroad.
She lives in Tokyo.

BANANA
YOSHIMOTO

Asleep

....

Translated from the Japanese

by Michael Emmerich

faber and faber

First published in the United States of America in 2000
by Grove Press, New York
First published in Great Britain in 2000
by Faber and Faber Limited
3 Queen Square London WC1N 3AU

This paperback edition first published in 2001

Printed in England by
Mackays of Chatham plc, Chatham, Kent

Originally published by Kadokawa Shoten as *Shirakawa Yofune*

This translation is based on the first edition of *Shirakawa Yofune,* but it
incorporates a few changes made by Yoshimoto for the Japanese
paperback edition

A CIP record for this book
is available from the British Library

ISBN 0-571-20537-2

10 9 8 7 6 5 4 3 2 1

THIS TRANSLATION IS DEDICATED TO ITŌ KIYO

Contents

Night and Night's Travelers

<hr />

Dear Sarah,
It was spring when we went to see my brother off.
He and his girlfriends were waiting at the airport
when we arrived—yes, he had lots of girlfriends
back then—and they were all decked out like
flowers. The sky was marvelously clear . . .

The flood of memories that streamed over me when this
draft of an old letter emerged from the depths of one of my
drawers was so powerful that for a few moments I stopped
cleaning and just sat still. I read through the English text again
and again, speaking the words aloud.

The letter was addressed to a young woman Yoshihiro
had dated when he was in high school. Her name was Sarah,
and she'd come to Japan as a student. Yoshihiro was my older
brother—he'd died a year ago. Almost as soon as Sarah went
back to Boston, Yoshihiro had begun talking about how he
wanted to see what it was like to live in some other country,
saying stuff like that, and then one day he just chased off after
her, hardly giving a moment's thought to what he was doing.
He worked various part-time jobs there and fooled around

doing a little of this and a little of that, and didn't come home for almost a year.

Yes . . . as I read the letter I remembered more and more about how things were back then. Yoshihiro had gone off so suddenly and contacted us so infrequently that Sarah had worried about it, and she had sent me a letter explaining how things were going in my brother's life. The letter I'd found was my reply to this. I'd been in high school when I wrote it, and it had never even crossed my mind that things might turn out the way they have. I was writing to a real American Girl—a very kind, very pretty American Girl. I flipped through the dictionary as I wrote, quivering with nervous excitement. Yes . . . Sarah was an adorable girl with intelligent blue eyes. Everything Japanese delighted her, and she was always trailing along behind my brother. She'd call his name. Yo-shi-hi-ro. Yo-shi-hi-ro. And her voice would overflow with an earnest love.

Sarah.

"If you can't do your English homework, get her to help."

Yoshihiro just tossed open the door to my room and said this: that's how casual an introduction he gave Sarah the first time he brought her to see me. She'd gone to the Summer Festival at a local shrine, and on her way home she'd stopped by our house. I happened to be sitting at my desk at the time, attempting to plow my way through several acres of summer homework, and since this sort of thing didn't happen every day, I had her write my English essay. She seemed so eager to help that I felt it would be unkind to refuse her. Really, I'm not lying. English had always been my best subject.

"I'll let you have her for an hour—but no more. After that I'll walk her home," Yoshihiro said. Then he went into the living room to watch TV.

"Sorry to spoil your date like this," I said in my rather wobbly English, and Sarah replied, "Hey, no problem. It'll take me about five minutes to get this done, and while I'm doing it you can be finishing up your work for some other subject, right?"—or words to that effect. Her English was smooth and easy, her voice was lovely, her blond hair seemed to be streaming down her head. She grinned.

"Well then—I guess if you could just make up something about 'A Day in My Life' and write it out, that would be terrific. If you make the sentences too complicated it'll be obvious that I got someone else to write it for me, so I'd appreciate it if you could make it more or less like the sample they give here," I said, struggling desperately to form these sentences, to make her understand.

"Okay. So what time do you get up every day? Do you have a Japanese-style breakfast? Or do you have bread? And what do you do in the afternoon?" She asked these and a few other questions, and suddenly we were finished.

I looked at the essay she'd written.

"Oh no! I can't turn it in like this—your handwriting is too good!" I cried. "I'll have to copy it out in my own ugly scrawl."

Sarah burst out laughing.

Thus, little by little, we began to loosen up, to start feeling comfortable with each other, and we spoke openly about all sorts of different things. The evening was slightly chilly, and the night air shivered with the shrilling of crickets. Sarah sat with one of her elbows propped up on a low table that I'd set out in the middle of my room, continuing to help with my homework. I found myself in a world of wonderful colors—colors that made it seem as if the entire room had been suddenly flooded with light. Blue and gold. Her white, almost transparent skin. The sharp line of her jaw as she gazed straight at me and nodded.

I thought of the black boat Commodore Perry arrived on when he came to "open" Japan. It was the first time I'd ever talked with someone from a foreign country at such close range, and she'd come whirling into my room so suddenly, so completely unexpectedly. I could hear the thump of drums and the sounds of flutes and a few other instruments out at the festival, ballooning along on the wind. Off in the distance a round moon drifted weightlessly up through the black sky. Every so often a soft breeze would slip in through the open window.

"Do you like Japan?"

"Yeah, I'm having a great time. And I've made lots of friends. Friends at school, and then Yoshihiro's friends. I don't think I'll ever forget this year."

"What do you like about my brother?"

"Yo-shi-hi-ro is like this giant ball of energy, you know—I just couldn't keep my eyes off him. I'm not just talking about some sort of physical energy. The thing I felt was something that came bubbling up from inside him, you know, something that will never run out, something extremely intellectual. I feel like just being with him makes it possible for me to keep changing, turning into something new, like I'll be able to make my way to someplace really far away, but in a way that's totally natural."

"What are you studying? Will you go back to school in Boston?"

"I'm studying Japanese culture. And I'll be going back a year from now. . . . It'll be hard for me to leave Yo-shi-hi-ro, but my parents are completely in love with Japan, they come over all the time, and then Yoshihiro has been saying that he'd like to come to the U.S. sometime, so I'm sure we'll meet again. Right now I'm putting every ounce of energy I have into studying Japanese. Except that for me, studying is basically just something I like to do—a kind of hobby. I'm sure I'll go on studying for the rest of my life, you know, but at the same time I really want to become a good mother, just like my mother. And for that reason I find Japanese women very interesting. I feel the same way about a lot of things as this Japanese Girl you hear so much about, I can sympathize with her more than I do with American girls. Because I think that certain parts of me aren't very American, you know? I guess eventually I'll end up marrying some businessman, maybe someone like my father, an international businessman. And then I want to put together a pleasant, bright, stable household."

"Do you think . . . I mean, it's possible my brother will become something international, but do you think he's got what it takes to be a businessman?"

"You're right, he doesn't. You get the feeling he'd be fired pretty quickly. They wouldn't like it that he's always thinking of himself."

"Of course he's still in high school, right? Maybe he'll change. I think it'd be great if he got interested in that kind of work. Maybe you could kind of steer him in that direction . . . ?"

This was a totally childlike thing to say, a thought even more distant than a dream. But Sarah was still enough of a child that she could have such dreams, and she had enough leeway to do so. The courage of a person who has no fear of the future. She laughed and then started to speak, with a look on her face like she was dreaming. Her eyes were those of someone who's just fallen in love, someone who sees nothing but her lover, someone who has no fear of anything. The eyes of someone who believes that every dream will come true, that reality will move if you just give it a push.

"Yeah, it would be awesome if it were Yoshihiro, wouldn't it? We could have one house in Japan and one in Boston, and go back and forth between the two. God, that would be so much fun! Because I really love Japan, you know, and if Yoshihiro got to like Boston then it'd be like we each had two countries, that's how we'd think about it! And then our little baby would grow up listening to the languages of two separate countries! And we would all go on trips together. It would be so fantastic. . . ."

Sarah belonged to a time so long ago that I never thought of her anymore, and I hadn't the slightest idea where she was or what she was doing—she was no longer part of my life. And then in the course of a perfectly ordinary day, as I was going about perfectly ordinary tasks, this letter appeared. It had been lying wadded into a hard little ball in the depths of my desk, in the dark recesses of a drawer I opened. Perhaps all this began when I plucked that wad out of the shadows, wondering what on earth it could be, and uncrinkled it with my fingers. As if some ancient spell had been broken, and was slowly dissolving, drifting out into the open air. . . .

Dear Sarah,
It was spring when we went to see my brother off.

He and his girlfriends were waiting at the airport when we arrived—yes, he had lots of girlfriends back then—and they were all decked out like flowers. The sky was marvelously clear, and my brother was in such a great mood, he was so delighted at the prospect of traveling that the rest of us got carried away too, and we were all happy and laughing. Those were good times. And we were all so glad that you and my brother were in love. It's strange, but somehow my brother just does that to people—all of

a sudden you find yourself seeing things the same
way he does. But of course you know that!

The cherry trees were in bloom when my
brother left. I remember seeing petals drifting down
here and there, like tiny flecks of light.

My brother doesn't write very often, but I
assume that means you're both doing well. I hope
you're having a nice time. Come visit us again in
Japan.

I look forward to our next meeting.

Shibami

Once, back when I was still a girl, my brother and I and our
cousin Mari went for a walk together along a dusk-darkened
road. Our relatives had gathered for a memorial service or something like that, and we'd gotten terribly bored and secretly
slipped away. We were just out wandering, we had no destination in mind.

The road stretched along one of the mounded-up banks
of a river near the house where my father had grown up. It was
that time of the evening, when off in the distance the other
bank of the river is just beginning to drop away into the darkness of night. Soon the halo of light that always hung over the
town at night would be reflected in the river, and even now
the clear air was gradually filling with indigo, the indigo air

drifted up, so that you almost felt as if you were seeing the air itself. The sky gleamed ever so faintly with the last traces of daylight, and everything was blurred, difficult to distinguish. Everything was beautiful.

I don't really remember what we'd been talking about, but I know that my brother said to me, "See, the problem with you is that you aren't bothered enough by what you might call the dirt of life."

As I recall, I'd been stating rather insistently that when I was an adult I was either going to be a businesswoman or else marry into some fabulously wealthy family, one or the other, that was absolutely definite, and if they wanted to know why, the reason was that our aunt Reiko—who'd married a businessman from a fabulously wealthy family—had looked simply gorgeous in her black dress, and because her genuine pearl necklace had been so splendid, and I was sure that if I could spend that kind of money on myself I'd look just as elegant as her.

My brother continued.

"Listen kiddo, by the time you grow up you'll have collected a whole lot of this 'dirt of life' stuff, right, you won't know where it's coming from but it'll pile up, and clothes and pearls won't look as beautiful to you as they do now—that's for sure. The problem is that dirt, see? You can't ever settle down in one place, you've got to live like you're always, always staring way off into the distance."

"Then how come you spend all your time at home?" I asked.

"You really do a great job of making things difficult, seeing as you know perfectly well what I'm talking about. I'm not talking about the body. Besides, you and I are still just kids, that's why we're still at home. Soon we'll be able to travel as far as we want to." Yoshihiro grinned.

And then Mari spoke, sounding dreamy. "Yeah, but I sure would love to marry someone rich . . ."

"God, the two of you just don't listen, do you?" My brother smiled peevishly.

"I mean I sort of understand what you're saying," Mari continued, "but I still think I'd rather just marry into some rich family. After all, I don't really like to travel around too much, and I've got lots of friends I don't want to leave."

Mari was three years older than me, and she already looked quite grown up. She could express what she was thinking very clearly, and she never hesitated at all when she spoke. "I just want to fall passionately in love with someone."

"What on earth are you talking about?" my brother said.

"Well, it's not likely that I'll end up leading a life that different from the one I'm leading now, is it? So there's nothing for me to do but fall passionately in love. Besides, I just love the idea of having everything fall to pieces. In the end you give in and slink off to get married to someone more appropriate. After all, these passionate love affairs always end badly," Mari said.

"I know what you mean," I said.

"You're a very strange young woman," my brother said.

Mari grinned. "But the best of all would be if you'd hurry up and get extraordinarily rich. Then as soon as my passionate love affair ends I can just slink on over to you. It'd be a really nice way of doing things, and since I know the sort of person you are I wouldn't have to worry about anything."

Even then my brother must have had that certain something that makes a man popular with women. He didn't even blush when our lovely older cousin teased him like this. He wasn't the slightest bit uncomfortable.

"It's true, isn't it. No hassle involved—nice and easy," he said.

"And I bet our parents would be thrilled, too."

"It'd be fun if we could live in the same house as you," I said.

Mari nodded, smiling slightly.

"But a lot of things are going to happen from now on," my brother said.

He sounded almost like he was talking to himself. I still find it strange. Why was it that even then, when he was still just a boy, my brother had such a profound if sketchy understanding of so much of life? Why did you get the impression that he already knew all about that mode of living where you're always making plans, always moving ahead, moving ahead, never settling down for good in any one place?

The three of us walked on and on along the bank of the river. The roar of the water crashed through the air with such thunderous force that it somehow ended up seeming very quiet.

Even so we were speaking quite loudly, and every little nothing we said seemed strangely pregnant with meaning.

I often remember that evening, the river flowing on into the distance.

And now a year had passed since my brother died.

*I*t really did snow a lot that winter. Maybe that explains why I hardly ever went out at night, but just stayed holed up inside my room. I was in college, but it had been decided that I'd study abroad the next semester, and that meant I didn't have to take any makeup exams. Which is to say that my situation ought have been very pleasant and carefree, but for no particular reason I'd gone and turned down every invitation I'd received to go skiing or to travel around spa-hopping. I guess maybe I'd gotten to like the feeling of being snowed in—maybe that explains it. All the plain old houses lining the plain old streets were dusted with white, so that it seemed like something out of science fiction. It was great. You felt like everything had come to a halt, like you were stuck in some sort of snowdrift where what had piled up wasn't snow but time.

It was snowing again that night. The snow kept streaming down outside, fast and thick, deepening. My parents had already gone to bed, and our cat was asleep—you couldn't hear a single living sound anywhere in the house. It was so quiet that I could even distinguish the low moan of the refrigerator out in the kitchen, and the rumble of cars driving along the main street.

I was reading a book, concentrating intently, so I didn't notice what was happening for quite some time. Then suddenly I glanced up, startled by the rapping I heard, and saw a white hand at the window, beating very precisely on the glass. The sight was so chilling it made the air in the room start to quake and quiver the way it does when you're listening to a ghost story. I was so shocked that I just sat there, not saying a word, staring at the window.

"Shibami! Hey!"

Mari's familiar voice and a string of giggles sounded faintly outside the window, muffled by the glass. I went over to the window and slid it open. Looking out, I saw a thoroughly snow-plastered Mari gazing up at me with a big smile on her face.

"God, you startled me," I said.

But even as I spoke I was having trouble accepting that Mari was there, suddenly there in front of me—I felt like I was dreaming. She'd been living with us until about three months earlier.

"Well then, I'll startle you even more."

She pointed to her feet. I focused my eyes on the dim rectangle of light that the window cast into the darkness, and realized that Mari wasn't wearing any shoes. I shrieked. All the time I was standing there gusts of snowy wind had been whirling around me into the room.

"Hurry inside. Go around to the front door," I said.

Mari nodded and walked off toward the front garden.

"What on earth have you been doing?" I asked her as soon as I'd given her a towel, and was setting the heater in the room on high. She'd been drenched when she stepped through the door, and her hands were so cold they seemed like they might be turning into ice.

Mari didn't say a word about how cold it was outside or about how warm it was inside or anything like that. She just grinned with her brilliant red cheeks and said, "Oh, nothing much."

She peeled off her wet socks and then sat down and put her bare feet up against the heater. Our cat slipped in through the crack between the door and the doorframe and came over and rubbed up against her. He'd always liked Mari. She started petting him, and I watched her, and gradually I began to understand. Mari was more or less a caged bird: she couldn't step out the front door of her house without first reporting to her parents. No doubt she'd been sitting by the window, gazing out at the snow, and suddenly she'd felt this urge to go outside, and since she didn't want to have to ask her parents for permission, she had just slipped out through the window. Luckily her room was on the first floor. . . .

Mari stood up. "You want some coffee?" she asked.

When I nodded she opened the door and strode off into the kitchen. The cat rolled himself up into a ball in the place Mari had been sitting, making it seem less and less obvious that she'd actually been there. As a matter of fact it had always been like that with Mari, even when she was living with us. She'd march through the house almost exactly the way a cat does, with that same air of belonging, and if you left her alone she'd just sit there staring off into space, not saying a word, or else go to sleep. You hardly even realized she was there. She seemed to be in the process of fading away.

That's not the way it used to be.

Mondays are English conversation, Tuesdays are swimming, Wednesdays she studies the tea ceremony, Thursdays she studies ikebana . . . that's the sort of feeling she had about her. She was the sort of person who was always doing something, and who did it all beautifully. In those days her very presence suffused a room with brightness and vigor. She wasn't an extraordinary beauty, but she had a really nice body, and her legs were long. Her features were all very compact and her face was tidily arranged, so the impression you got, looking at her, was one of cleanliness and purity. Whereas now she just seemed subdued. And I didn't think this was because she'd stopped using mascara and rouge, or because she was now twenty-five years old.

Mari had stopped responding to the outside world, she'd pulled the plug on the whole system, she was taking a break— I felt convinced of this. Because, as she saw things right now, life was nothing but pain.

"Here you go. One coffee with milk." Smiling, Mari held out a cup, rousing me from my thoughts.

"Thanks," I said.

She held a cup of strong black coffee in her hand, just like old times.

She kept grinning.

"Are you planning to stay over tonight?" I asked.

We'd left Mari's room in pretty much the same condition it had been in when she was living with us, and used it as a guest room. Though she hadn't read very many books during that period, and she hardly ever went out, and she hadn't listened to much music—basically all she did was go to sleep and then get up again, like a guest at some hotel who wasn't even having meals.

Mari shook her head. "No, I'll go back home. It'd only cause a big stir if my parents found out, so I'll go back before they do. I just had this urge to talk to someone, you know, and I figured you'd probably still be awake."

"Then I'll lend you some shoes before you head back," I said. "What was it you wanted to talk about?"

"Nothing, really. Actually I feel better already," Mari said.

Since it was late we both kept our voices down. As a result you almost had the feeling you could hear the snow whirling down outside. Snowflakes skittered whitely through the darkness on the far side of the fogged-up window. Everything seemed to gleam with a pale light.

"This sure is some snow," I said.

"Yeah, I bet it'll pile up tonight."

Mari's tone of voice made it sound like none of it really mattered much to her. For someone who'd just come walking barefoot over asphalt through the pitch black, she seemed pretty indifferent to the cold. I looked at her profile, her long hair, her small round lips. She was flipping disinterestedly through some new magazine.

I walked her as far as the front gate when she left.

The snow really was incredible—it hopped around cha-otically right in front of your eyes, like it was dancing. The street just in front of our house was lost in the darkness and the snow. You could hardly even make it out.

"Hey," Mari said, laughing. "Wouldn't it be chilling if you got a notice tomorrow morning saying that I'd died some-time late tonight? Don't you think maybe I'm really a ghost?"

"Don't even say stuff like that! I'll be up all night, you know, all alone!"

I'd practically shouted this. But it was true, I'd been thinking all along that this was an awfully spooky situation—almost like a haunting.

A barefoot cousin who bangs on the window late one snowy night.

"Which reminds me, I had a dream about Yoshihiro yesterday afternoon," Mari said. "It was the first time I'd dreamt about him in ages."

She'd taken a pair of bright red gloves out of her pocket, and as she spoke she slipped her hands into them, clomping her feet around in the much-too-big shoes I'd lent her. Her clear voice glittered in the night; the air was so cold it felt like pinpricks.

"It's been months since I dreamt of him, seriously. In the dream I only saw his back, and he was wearing that jacket—the black one. I was walking down some street when I noticed that there was a back I sort of recognized, up ahead of me, in the middle of a crowd of people. So I'm thinking, *Who can that be? Who on earth can that be?* And then I decide to go find out, right, so I chase after him. And as I get closer and closer I start feeling so confused and so nervous that my chest starts to ache. I'm really upset. That back seems to be so precious to me. I don't exactly understand why, somehow it just seems precious to me. So precious that I want to hurl myself onto it and hold it tight and squeeze it to a pulp. And then all of a sudden, just as I'm about to lay my hand on his shoulder, I remember his name. 'Yoshihiro!' I actually called his name. And that woke me up. I was sleeping on the sofa in the living room, you know, and I shouted so loudly that my mother came in from one of the rooms in the back of the house and asked if I'd called. I told her I'd had a really scary dream. And it's true, isn't it? It really is scary."

Having said this, she waved and called good-bye, smiling.

And then she vanished into the snow.

Something about my brother's tone of voice when he called us up long-distance to tell us that he'd be returning immediately to Japan told me that things were over between him and Sarah. I didn't know what had happened. I just had a feeling that things were over.

"There's nothing keeping me anymore. I'm coming home," he said.

"You want me to come meet you at the airport?" I asked.

I had the idea it might be very relaxing to cut school and go to Narita.

"Sure, if you've got nothing else to do. I'll treat you to lunch."

"You don't have to do that. My schedule's open. Is there anyone you want me to ask along? How about those girls who came to see you off?"

My brother's voice reached me through static.

"Actually . . . could you ask Mari?"

Mari.

For a moment I wasn't able to connect the name my brother had said with the person—our cousin, Mari. I struggled to think who he could mean.

"Mari? Why her?"

"She's sent me some letters, you know, and then six months ago she came to Boston. She and Sarah and I had dinner together. Just give her a call, okay?"

I realized then that my brother was starting to fall for Mari. He wasn't even trying to hide it. He'd just come right out and given me her name.

In fact there had been something between them ever since they were small, something that pulled them together even when they were paying no attention to each other at all. Something that would probably make them fall in love sooner or later. As they got older, each time they fell in love with someone else, that something became increasingly concentrated.

I called Mari and asked if she wanted to go to Narita. She said she'd go. She explained that she'd stopped by Boston on her way back to Japan when she made a trip to New York.

"We had dinner one night. The three of us, him and Sarah and me. Sarah had really changed. She was terribly thin, and very adult, and she didn't say very much. She didn't smile at all. Yoshihiro was just like he always is, just as cheery as always, and you had the feeling that he just went on being the same Yoshihiro no matter whether he was in Japan or Boston. You felt that in the way he acted toward Sarah, too. But Sarah looked completely worn out. Just Sarah. I'm not sure why. I just know that I had the feeling that things were over between them. . . . It bothered me, so I wrote Yoshihiro a letter when I got back to Japan. But the letter I got in reply was just a regular letter. Sarah's doing very well, and she's a really nice girl, and I sure do miss Japan, and I'm dying for a taste of cod roe, that kind of thing. I remember thinking, *God, Yoshihiro's a really great guy.* And that's really how I felt. He'd never say anything bad about Sarah to me, the girl who'd sat there surrounded by Boston's clear night air, staring right at him, the girl who'd started liking him. I'd gotten sort of drunk on all that traveling, but when I got that letter I thought about things again, and I felt like some of the dirt I'd had inside me had been washed away, just a little, and so I sent him a postcard apologizing. He really is a good guy."

When the time came I got my boyfriend to take us in his car.

We picked up Mari and headed for the airport.

It was a beautiful, slightly chilly autumn day. The kind of afternoon when invisible rays of sun stream down through the glass into the airport lobby. The plane arrived a little late, and there was an announcement saying that it had landed, and then finally, little by little, the passengers began to emerge.

Mari's long hair was tugged back into a ponytail, and she had the band wound extremely tightly. She acted so jittery you got the feeling she must be just as taut inside. She looked like her heart must be close to bursting.

"Mari . . . what's wrong?" I asked.

"I wish I knew," she said.

A blue sweater and a tight beige skirt. The white of the lobby's floor set the colors off marvelously. She stood by herself, like the star of some movie, her pretty, tidily arranged face turned so that I saw it in profile, and she was staring so fixedly at the monitor that she almost seemed to be ripping into it with her eyes. Looking at her, you had the feeling that she existed in some way more real than any of the other people in the crowds waiting for the plane—that she more thoroughly filled the space she occupied. My brother didn't come out. Little scenes began playing themselves out all around us. People coming back together. And then the line of emerging passengers dribbled away into nothing. I took my boyfriend's hand in mine. "He sure is taking his time," I said. But to tell the truth I wasn't looking at the monitor or even at the line—I was watching Mari. I was staring at her, at that figure standing there, so lovely it seemed she might shatter everything. Then my brother finally emerged, pushing a big trunk, looking like he'd matured a whole lot, and Mari started moving toward him through the crowds, walking fast, strangely fast, as if she were walking through a dream. Yoshihiro's face looked a little more tired than it had the day we'd come to see him off. Little by little she drew closer to him.

"Hey!" Yoshihiro spotted us all and waved.

Then he looked straight at Mari. "Mari. It's been a while."

She smiled faintly. "Welcome back, Yoshihiro," she said.

Her voice merged with the hustle and bustle of the lobby. It sounded very low when it reached my ears, and more adult than I'd ever known it.

"Are they going out or something?" asked my boyfriend.

He didn't know anything about the two of them, and I figured that since things seemed to be heading in that direction anyway, I might as well just say they were. So I nodded. Mari was telling my brother that there were all kinds of things she'd been wanting to talk over with him. I went on watching her as she spoke. My brother nodded. Then he put his hand around her shoulder.

"Did Mari come by last night, fairly late?"

We were sitting at the breakfast table when my mother said this.

"Yes. How'd you know?" I replied, surprised.

"I got up in the middle of the night to go to the bathroom, and she was in the kitchen making coffee, doing it in the pitch dark. I was still half asleep, you know, feeling a little vague, and it totally slipped my mind that she isn't living with us anymore. So I just said, 'My goodness, are you still up?' And then she said that she was and grinned at me, so I didn't think anything of it, and I just went back to our room and fell asleep again. So it wasn't a dream, then?"

"Nope," I said. "She was here. She just showed up all of a sudden."

Sunlight poured down out of the cloudless sky and smacked onto the thick accumulation of snow, making the space beyond the window so dazzling that it looked utterly new and clean. A peculiar feeling came over me as I gazed into that light, a feeling like I wanted to get some more sleep, like I was irritated about something. The television was bawling out the morning news, flooding the room with energy. My mother had sent my father off to work ages ago, and we were having a late breakfast together.

"Maybe things aren't going too well in her other house?" my mother said.

"Her other house? Mom, that 'other house' is her real house. She actually has a mother and father of her own, you know, real parents."

I laughed. I knew what my mother meant.

"I really got to like her while she was living with us," she said.

BANANA YOSHIMOTO

My mother never even mentioned my brother anymore. Instead she'd spent the last year taking special care of Mari, trying to distract herself that way. Sometimes I'd find myself wondering what all this must seem like to her, what sort of terrible fantasy it must feel like. Giving birth to a son like him, bringing him up, then losing him. I just couldn't imagine it at all. "Mmhm," I said, nodding, and went on nibbling at my bread. Mari had spent her whole time in our house with my mother, helping out with the housework and carrying around shopping bags and doing all sorts of stuff like that. There wasn't much else for her to do, and it was probably pretty effective in helping her to keep her spirits up. Yet as much as she pitched in like one of the family, she still always gave a little smile at dinner and said how delicious everything was, and whenever she and one of us happened to want a bath at the same time, she'd always say very politely that she'd wait until later, and gesture for you to go first, displaying the palm of her hand. She'd been very carefully brought up, and her manners impressed me very much. But she wasn't really living in our house, she wasn't really alive. She just stayed there in the same space with us, a pleasant presence, like a resident ghost. She existed like a mirage.

The only time I really felt vividly aware that Mari was a living creature during the time she stayed in our house was when she was crying. Even that didn't happen too often during the second half of her stay, but in the beginning, during the weeks after she first came to live with us, she'd always be sobbing to

26

herself in the guest room when I went into the kitchen to make coffee at night. Her sobs slipped softly through the darkness and sank down into me, into my very being, the way the endless rains do in the monsoon season.

I often got pretty depressed myself back then. It felt like I was standing at the very edge of this world, that's the kind of mood I was in, the kind of emptiness I felt. And in those days, whenever Mari was all alone in the house, when everyone else had gone out, she'd slip into my brother's bedroom—his room, which we'd left just as it was when he died. I'd notice that she was gone when I came home, and I'd get a little worried and would go upstairs and catch sight of her through the half-open door, curled up in the middle of my brother's color-filled room, crying. She even cried in the bath. I'd head for the bathroom as soon as she'd finished, planning to take a bath myself, and when we passed in the hall, steam would still be rising from her skin; her face would be a brilliant red, you could tell she'd just climbed up out of the hot water . . . and yet her eyes would be red and puffy, and she'd be sniffling as she walked by. *It wouldn't surprise me to discover that she left the water salty,* I'd think as I lowered myself into the bathtub, and then I'd sit with the hot steam drifting up all around me, feeling so terrible that I could hardly stand it.

Could it actually be true that tears help people to heal?

Because Mari did eventually stop crying, and went back home.

"Ask her to come when we can talk next time, okay? I mean, if you should happen to run into her someplace," my mother said.

"Okay, I'll tell her if I see her," I replied, standing up.

I went to campus and handed in a few essays, then decided that maybe it wouldn't be such a bad idea to clean out my locker every once in a while, and went over to the locker room. When I got there I found a note taped to the door. I took it down and read it. It was from a friend, a guy named Ken'ichi.

> I can return the money.
> Call me around lunchtime tomorrow.
>
> > Ken'ichi

Ken'ichi had borrowed money from practically every bozo in the world and then run off without returning a yen to anyone. He had stopped coming to campus a while ago. I'd lent him fifty thousand yen all together, but I hadn't actually expected to get any of it back. My brother was the same way, so I could sort of understand. Judging from the things I heard, it sounded like you'd come up with a pretty incredible sum if you added up all the money he'd managed to scrape together, and so everyone was raging, people were going crazy with anger. But even though there were occasions when I'd find myself staring at some piece of clothing I'd wanted, thinking,

If only I had that fifty thousand yen right now, I just figured that was the way things went. He was a good guy, but that didn't mean anything when it came to money. *And anyway, who could stand to be around someone who wasn't just a good guy, but even returned your money on time?* I thought, shaking my head, wondering how he could possibly manage to pay me back. I folded up the note and put it in my pocket, then headed out into the still-snowy courtyard.

"Hey Shibami!" someone called.

I turned toward the voice, and saw that Tanaka was standing nearby.

"Hey, has Ken'ichi said anything about paying you back?" I asked.

I'd heard that Tanaka had lent money to Ken'ichi too.

"No, he hasn't! And it's no joke, either—I lent the jerk thirty thousand yen! I can't believe he'd use my money to run off to Hawaii with some girl!"

He sounded pretty seriously enraged.

"Hawaii?"

"Yeah. He's dating some high school kid."

"Really? And has he come back?"

"You think I'd know?"

"Oh."

How like him. I bet he's only planning to pay back the people he likes.

I nodded in agreement with myself as I thought this.

"Why? Have you heard from him?" asked Tanaka.

"Nope, not a word!" I said, shaking my head. I certainly didn't want to make things difficult for Ken'ichi now that he'd said he was going to pay me back.

"By the way, I've been seeing your cousin around a lot lately."

"What do you mean? Around where?" I asked.

Mari and Tanaka were acquaintances.

"What do you mean, where? That bar by the intersection, the one that's open all night, and over at the side of the road, and at Denny's, you know, in this area basically, usually at night."

"I see—at night." I nodded. So the previous night's excursion hadn't just been a onetime affair. Yes . . . come to think of it, she'd lacked the vigor of someone out enjoying the night. She'd been wandering around in a trance, like a sleepwalker.

What did she see on that snow-blanketed night, as she stood gazing up at the light streaming from my window? Perhaps since it was so dark outdoors the interior of my room looked extremely bright, very white. Perhaps it looked like it would be really warm and cozy inside?

These thoughts made me feel a little sad.

I said good-bye to Tanaka, and we walked off in opposite directions.

On my way home from work I stopped by the place Tanaka had mentioned, that dark and rather somber bar, hoping to meet up with Mari. It was pretty dimly lit inside, too, but what got to you most was the gloominess of the neighborhood. The place is directly across from a cemetery.

Mari was there. She had her elbows propped up on her table.

I walked over, calling her name.

"Hey, what luck!" she said.

She pointed at a bag lying on the chair next to her.

I sat down across from her. "What do you mean? What's so lucky?"

"Your shoes are in there."

"Are they?" I smiled.

"Yup." Mari smiled back.

Then she held out the bag, a gorgeous one from the expensive department store Isetan. No doubt my scuffed-up shoes were sitting in a beautiful box inside that bag, carefully dried and rubbed until they were clean. It occurred to me that the elegant way Mari had of going about things like this was the lingering effect of certain habits she'd developed in a past that was now lost to her—that those habits were controlling her actions even now. I felt a kind of tenderness as I sat staring at her, the sort of feeling you might have looking at a ghost.

"So you'd been planning to stop by our house?" I asked.

"Yeah. But since the windows were dark, I decided to just go home."

I ordered a gin and tonic, and told her what my mother had said.

"My mother says to come visit during the day. She says it's like she's dreaming you when you come at night, so it isn't any fun."

Mari burst out laughing. "I knew it! She was still half asleep then, right? The stuff she was saying was kind of crazy, you know, so I just played along with her."

"That's what she said," I said.

For some time we sat and drank in silence. Mari was gazing out at the river of cars flowing past outside the window, her eyes open incredibly wide. Her expression didn't seem especially unhappy, and yet I recalled that when she was a girl she'd had a real aversion to the nighttime, and that she couldn't stand to stay up late: even when we stayed over at one or the other of our houses she'd always go to sleep once it passed ten o'clock. And as soon as I started thinking about these things—even though she was my cousin, a cousin I'd known for ages—she started to seem like someone new, like someone who'd changed in ways I knew absolutely nothing about.

"Did you know that Sarah was pregnant?" Mari said suddenly.

"Huh?" For a moment this was the only reply I could make. I was trying to pluck the words "Sarah" and "pregnant" out from among all the other words in my head, trying to put them together. Finally I understood.

"No, I had no idea!" I said.

"Yeah, I guess I just remembered it myself, you know, all of a sudden. You know how in places like this where it's dark and there's music playing real loud, suddenly you find yourself sort of vaguely remembering all kinds of things that you'd forgotten? You know what I mean? And then there's that blue-eyed girl at the table over there, right? She's been there for quite a while. So I started wondering what Sarah's doing these days. . . ."

"Was it my brother's?"

"As a matter of fact, she said she didn't know." Mari burst out laughing. "You see, Sarah had been having her cake and eating it, too, for quite some time. She was dating an old child-hood pal from Boston at the same time she was dating Yoshihiro. It's like these stories you hear about guys who live out in the country having one girlfriend at college and one back at home, you know? Sarah was doing the same thing, except that hers was the international version. Apparently Yoshihiro only found out about all that after he'd arrived in Boston. And of course he was Japanese, right? So he knew that he'd eventually go back to Japan, and from what I can tell it seems like he drew back from her on his own. But Sarah kept him from going. So for the last six months the three of them were totally tangled up, evidently it was all a huge mess. And Yoshihiro really didn't like that kind of mess, right, and so he was probably running away the whole time, that's probably how he made it through, except that when you're overseas—I mean, there probably wasn't anywhere for him to run, was there? He didn't have anyone he could turn to, after all. But then you think about Sarah—how she got to know Yoshihiro just after she'd arrived in Japan, and how she grew to like him a whole lot . . . I'm sure that must have been terribly hard for her, too. Back then, back before there was anything between Yoshihiro and me, she used to talk to me about all that fairly often. About how she already had a steady boyfriend in Boston, and about how she did like Yo-shi-hi-ro a whole lot, except that the two of them were from different countries, and though for the time being she was here studying in Japan she'd eventually be going back, and about how hard that would be. That kind of thing. Yoshihiro said he didn't know whether Sarah's pregnancy was real or whether it was just a big put-on, but that even if it was true, which seemed kind of unlikely, it was almost definitely the other guy's child. That's what he said."

"I had no idea about any of this," I said.

But even as I said this I was putting certain things together.

Of course the pregnancy wasn't the only thing I hadn't known about. I'd never even been told that Sarah had a boyfriend in Boston. That day Sarah and I had talked—had that dream she'd told me about been something she only wished for when she was in Japan, something she only told me about because I happened to be her boyfriend's kid sister? Maybe she wanted to act out the role of the older brother's perfect girlfriend for me, just for me, the innocent sibling? I remembered the way her translucent golden bangs had looked as she did my homework for me. Her unclouded eyes. No, that hadn't been it. She'd really meant what she was saying. The sparkle in her eyes told me that she really wanted to believe everything would work out all right. . . . Or maybe her boyfriend in Boston was the sort of businessman type that she had described to me. Could it be that all my brother did was put a little twist in Sarah's life, and then vanish?

Thinking about it wouldn't help me understand. The only thing I understood about Sarah was that she had been an adult then. She'd been more of an adult than me, more of an adult than my brother, more of an adult than Mari. She'd been so grown up I felt sorry for her.

I was drunk now. The darkness of the bar seemed so incredibly still and settled that it startled me. And yet Mari seemed more sharply visible than anyone else, the outline of her form even clearer than that of the dismal-looking young waitress chatting with a customer at the bar on the other side of the room, clearer than that of the stunningly gorgeous woman with the long hair who was sitting with her boyfriend, holding her head close to his, and clearer than that of the woman with the childlike features sitting by the window, smoking a cigarette and looking at a magazine. Why was it that Mari appeared this way? I considered the matter vaguely.

"So . . . is Sarah back in Japan now?" Mari asked.

"What do you mean?" I said, startled. "She only came to Japan to study, right? And that was years ago. She didn't even come back when Yoshihiro died!"

Mari's expression softened. No doubt my reaction had made it perfectly clear to her that I wasn't hiding Sarah's return to Japan from her, trying to make things easy.

35

"You see, I got this mysterious phone call yesterday," she said.

"Mysterious in what way?"

"Well, when I picked up the phone and said hello there was no response—just silence. So I kept listening for a while, right, and then I heard this guy's voice in the background, speaking in English. Of course it might just have been a prank call— maybe the person had the public-radio English Conversation Seminar going in the background or something—but I don't know . . . the density of that silence . . . it was like whoever it was was about to start speaking, but couldn't make up her mind to do it, you know, that sort of silence. So I kind of got the idea that it might be Sarah. That's all."

"I see," I said.

To tell the truth, right then I wasn't the slightest bit concerned about Sarah and whether it had been her calling. More than anything, it frightened me that Mari was talking about these things—things related to my brother, who'd been dead for so long—as if it were all perfectly ordinary, part of everyday life.

"I'll let you know if I hear anything."

"Good, I hope you do," Mari said, and smiled.

When we parted, Mari called out her good-bye in a voice so incredibly loud you'd have thought it was the middle of the day, and then walked briskly off. I listened for a moment to the sound of her shoes scraping across the asphalt, and then started walking down the night-dark road myself.

★ ★ ★

*W*hen I was in junior high school my mother found out that my father was having an affair. There was a huge commotion at home, and in the end both my parents left the house. It was the middle of winter.

The affair was probably just a tiny little fling, the sort of thing people have all the time, but my mother went into hysterics and ran off to her parents' house, leaving me and my brother behind. My father went to bring her back. Evidently their talks didn't go very well, things got complicated . . . but it would be totally wrong to suppose that my brother and I were even the slightest bit confounded at being left on our own. The first thing we did was get Mari to come stay with us. Next we took advantage of all the confusion to withdraw huge loads of cash with our parents' ATM card and buy anything and everything that we'd been wanting. We stayed up until very late every night drinking booze. Mari was just eighteen, but in my eyes she was already a beautiful adult woman.

Come to think of it, the three of us slept side by side then.

It was snowing that evening too, and it was terribly cold— the sort of night where you couldn't even make yourself get up to go to the bathroom. Outside the window, the air was so bitterly cold you almost expected it to snap suddenly into a single frozen block. That frigid air, pushing up against the window. . . .

But inside the room it was warm, and we were all drunk and completely stuffed. That night we slept in our clothes, lying under the kotatsu. My brother was the first to drift off, his breathing becoming slow and steady and deep. Then Mari, already half dozing, settled down. I was so incredibly sleepy myself that I could hardly stand it anymore, and so without saying a word I lay down beside her. Our eyes met. "Why don't we just sleep here tonight," Mari said. And then she lifted the upper half of her body and bent down over Yoshihiro's cheek and gave him a kiss good night. I goggled at her, startled. She grinned and gave me a kiss too, one that lasted just as long as my brother's.

"Thank you," I said. Mari answered with a little smile, then flopped artlessly down and shut her eyes. Snow hurtled without a sound into the depths of the night, streaming down all around, closing us in. I went to sleep staring at the shadows that Mari's long eyelashes cast on her white skin.

Our parents finally returned after four days to find the entire house turned upside down, and the three of us all dressed up in fancy clothes that they'd never seen before, suffering from the lingering effects of the previous night's drinking. They were pretty shocked, and they gave my brother an earful: he was older than me, and had been more or less responsible for everything.

But Yoshihiro didn't give in. "The idea that the two of you might split up scared me so much that I didn't know what else to do!" he said, making our parents cry. It was unbelievably fun.

The night glittered brilliantly then. The night seemed to be infinitely long. And I could see something stretching way off into the distance behind Yoshihiro, whose eyes sparkled with the same mischievous light as always. I caught sight of a vast landscape.

Something like a panorama.

I kind of wonder if that wasn't The Future, as my childish heart saw it. Back then my brother was something that definitely wouldn't die, he was both night and something that traveled through night—something like that.

Yes. And during the last part of his life he hardly spent any time at home, so he wasn't what he'd been for me when he was small. He became the equivalent of a stranger.

But when I'd been talking with Mari like this, or when it got unbearably hot in the summer and my whole family started complaining and we set all the air conditioners in the house on high, or when night had fallen and there was a typhoon raging outside—at times like that, I'd think of Yoshihiro, and I'd yearn to have him back with us. It was like that even while he was alive. It didn't matter whether he was nearby or far away. His image would drift up into your mind just when you least expected it, shocking you, making your chest pound. Making your heart ache.

*E*arly in the morning the phone rang.

Our telephone is right next to the door to my room, so I wandered out, still half asleep, and lifted the receiver.

"Hello?" I said.

I heard a little gasp on the other end of the phone—a woman's startled exclamation. Maybe this was Sarah, just like Mari had said? I tried to fit the gasp I'd heard with the distant memories I had of Sarah's voice, but in the end I couldn't tell whether it was her or not. It seemed sort of like her, but at the same time I had the feeling it wasn't.

"Sarah?" I said.

There was a brief space of silence, a feeling that the line was about to go dead. A silence that was neither denial nor affirmation.

I'd only just been buffeted out of sleep, and still couldn't think very clearly. My legs seemed wobbly, and various half-formed thoughts were spiraling around in my head, whirlpool-like.

Suppose Sarah's in Japan now, and suppose there's some reason why she can't come and talk freely, out in the open, and that she feels it's too late now even to tell me who she is. Suppose she just wants to make sure that we're still here, that her old friends are still here.

But these were only speculations. The silence told me nothing.

"Sarah—wait," I said.

From the depths of an ocean of sleepiness, in my barely adequate English. The line didn't go dead. And so I continued.

"This is Shibami, Yoshihiro's sister.

"We met a couple of times, and we've exchanged letters.

"I'm twenty-two now.

"I'm sure you've changed a lot too.

"Maybe there's nothing linking us anymore, but some-where deep down inside I'm always thinking of you.

"The other day I found a draft of a letter I wrote you, and I was thinking about the time you did my homework for me—letting myself remember."

When I stopped speaking I heard the faintest trace of a commotion on the other end of the line. A clamorous barrage of voices, as if a crowd of people was passing by in the background. Then it was silent again. And then, gradually, the sound of someone sobbing reached my ear, a tear-filled gasping that grew steadily louder and stronger. I shuddered.

"Sarah?" I said.

Sarah was crying. "I'm sorry. . . ."

The voice was faint, but it was definitely hers.

All right! We'll be able to talk!

"Sarah, are you in Japan?" I asked.

"Yes, but I can't come to see you," Sarah said.

"Have you come with someone? A man? Aren't you able to call me from your room? You're in a hotel now, right?"

Sarah didn't answer. She just went on crying.

Then she spoke. "I just wanted to know how you're doing. Hearing your voice . . . everything came back to me, I remembered being in your house . . . how much fun it was being in Japan."

"Are you happy now?" I asked.

"Yes. Actually I'm married."

For the first time, Sarah laughed. "I'm fine, I'm really not unhappy. You don't have to worry."

"Well, that's all right, then. I'm glad," I said.

Suddenly Sarah changed the subject. "Tell me, Shi-ba-mi. Was Yo-shi-hi-ro alone when he died? I mean, I'm wondering if he had a true love, you know? I just want to know that."

I realized that Sarah must have felt it back then. It must have been already apparent by the time Mari went to Boston—it must have been visible in the color of her eyes, and in my brother's gaze. Because he always had a peculiar light in his eyes when he looked at Mari. As if he was calming himself, clearing his mind, confirming that what he saw was true. Making sure that she was actually alive and moving. That she was really there, really laughing.

She must have sensed all that.

"Yes, he was still alone," I said.

I put every ounce of strength I had into that lie.

"He had female friends, but there was no one you could call his true love."

"I see. . . . " Sarah said. "Sorry to ask such a terrible question. I'm afraid I've kind of been losing it since I arrived in Japan. But I'm happy that we were able to talk. Thanks to you, of course."

This was no longer the Sarah who was unable to stop herself from making phone calls and then not saying a word, who was hurt so much by her memories that she ended up crying. This was the levelheaded Sarah I knew.

"Well, take care. I've got to go back to the room," Sarah said.

"Okay. . . . Good-bye then," I replied.

I was now totally awake. The patch of sky visible through the window was a strange wash of subtle gradations of cloud and blue, and the interior of the room was very bright. Somehow that brightness felt terribly sad.

What strange weather, I thought.

"Sarah, I hope you'll be happy—I really hope you'll be happy!"

"Thanks, Shi-ba-mi," Sarah said.

And then the line went dead.

I settled into a strange mood—it felt as if I'd seen something through to its conclusion, but at the same time I felt overwhelmingly sad. It occurred to me once again how incredible Mari was. To think she'd figured out that Sarah was back in Japan just from listening to a silent phone call! There hadn't been the slightest hint of uncertainty in her eyes when she told me it was Sarah. She had known. Yes . . . perhaps Mari, wandering in the interval between dream and reality as she was, perhaps she could sense that much, figure out who was calling almost before she knew it, feel it as clearly as something she held cupped in her hand.

★ ★ ★

I called Ken'ichi later that day. He'd promised to pay me back today.

"Hello?"

"Hey—is that you, Shibami?"

"Is it true that you're going to pay me back?"

"Yep. I've earned a bit of money, and I'm going to return every yen."

"I hear you used my savings to go to Hawaii."

"Hawaii? Are you kidding? It was Atami, not Hawaii!"

"Oh? Everyone's been saying you went to Hawaii."

"I suppose they probably added up all the money I'd gotten from everyone and just picked a destination based on the cost. Asses. I certainly won't be giving that Tanaka any of his money back."

"So what is it with Atami? Why there?"

"I'll tell you about it later. Where should we meet? I'll let you decide."

"The lobby of the K. Hotel at one o'clock," I said.

I'd heard at some point that Sarah's parents usually stayed at the K. Hotel when they came to Japan, and it had occurred to me that Sarah might stay there too. I had put a call through to the front desk earlier and given them Sarah's name, but they said that as far as they could tell, no one by that name was staying there. Yet I hadn't been able to give up hope completely.

"Okay," Ken'ichi said.

And he hung up.

★ ★ ★

*T*he lobbies of these giant hotels always feel deserted. It doesn't matter how crowded they really are; the feeling is a fundamental part of these places, it drifts through every corner. Evidently Ken'ichi hadn't shown up yet. I sank down into the thick cushions of one of the couches and glanced around.

I didn't have a chance of finding Sarah. The place was awash with foreigners. Of course most of them were suit-clad businessmen: their buttery-smooth English swooped around under the high ceiling, sounding exactly like music . . . I started feeling more and more dazed.

I finally spotted Ken'ichi through the glass door, coming my way.

He stopped in front of my couch and held out an envelope. "Here's the money."

I took the envelope in silence. I certainly couldn't thank him.

"Have you got some time now?"

"Yeah, I'm pretty much free."

"Well then, I'll buy you some tea," Ken'ichi said.

He sat down across from me.

As we were drinking our tea he smiled and said, "People and their rumors sure are frightening, aren't they? Hawaii, indeed! I wish I could go to Hawaii."

"So what did you do with the five hundred thousand yen? Not that you have to tell me if you don't want to."

"It's fine with me. We went on this terrifically lavish vacation in Atami. Went around to all the very best old Japanese

45

inns, you know, and ate delicious foods every day, and drove around to various places. We stayed for two weeks. Look at my skin. Super sleek, no? Not a surprise, I guess, after so much luxury."

"You went with your girlfriend?"

"Yeah."

"I hear she's in high school," I said, smiling. "Unbelievable."

With that Ken'ichi exploded into laughter.

"What are you talking about! She's in a two-year college. It's amazing, the completely ridiculous rumors that people start! Maybe I ought to keep myself out of sight a little longer—I'd love to see just how overblown this thing gets!"

"Yeah, that's how it goes with rumors. You don't pay people back, so it just gets more and more extreme. But seriously—is there that much stuff to do at Atami? It seems like it'd get boring, even for lovers."

"But having all that time is what's so nice. . . . Or rather, anything would have been okay as long as it was somewhere far away from everyday life. You see, my girlfriend's parents are 'newly-divorceds,' as it were, and the whole situation is really rough, so I wanted to take her away from all that, you know? Except that traveling overseas wears you down, and Atami has all those old spas, and I'd heard that you never get bored there—it seemed like the perfect place. It was great to make plans like that, but I had no money. Not a single yen."

Ken'ichi burst out laughing again.

"I see," I said.

"When people start getting depressed there's just no end to it—things just seem to get worse and worse. And I'd start getting drawn into it myself when I was with her, you know, so that I ended up becoming a little weird too. Of course, things did seem to be pretty horrendous in her house, so there wasn't much anyone could do. For instance, say we'd arranged to meet somewhere. And say I showed up about fifteen minutes late, just like I always do. Well, she'd already be all listless and droopy. And then she'd cry. I don't know, it's not like we even got together that much in the first place, but all of a sudden even I got this urge to go do something fun, you know? Of course I don't know how much fun it was for her, but I definitely had a good time."

"Sounds reasonable," I said.

Then I smiled.

*E*vidently even Mari and my brother hadn't realized how strongly Mari's parents would object to their relationship. But if I think things over, I can see that if I were a parent with an only daughter, and if I'd paid good money so that she could learn to play the piano and take English Conversation classes and all that, I definitely wouldn't want to let her go off with a guy who looked as much like a womanizer as my brother.

I saw the two of them during the days when their love for each other first began to deepen, unknown to anyone, and I watched them during the days after people found out and started putting pressure on them to end the relationship, when

47

they dated in secret. The difference between those two environments was as enormous as that between light and dark. But since my brother was the sort of person who could find pleasure in the very enormity of that difference, and since Mari was the sort of person who was thrilled by anything that she did without telling her parents, and who delighted in that thrill, the two of them seemed to be fairly happy.

*T*he phone would ring twice and then stop.

This was Mari's signal for my brother to call her.

Hearing it and heading for the phone. His sweet steps.

*Y*oshihiro got in a car accident and died in the emergency room of the hospital. He'd been on his way to a rendezvous with Mari when the accident happened, so he'd kept the date a secret from the rest of us. Our father worked as a surgeon at a very big hospital, so if we'd known where he'd been headed we could have had him rushed straight there, and it's possible that he might have been saved.

Could any story leave you with an aftertaste as unpleasant as this one? I think the reason Mari got so terribly depressed was that it happened while she was waiting. She was waiting in a café just across from the train station. It was a very bright shop that everyone used as a meeting place. She got any number of refills on her coffee, ate two pieces of cake, drank a lemon soda, had some ice cream. . . . She waited for five hours. Then she trudged back to her house and was informed of her lover's death.

She told me about it much later.

"It felt like the inside of my stomach had turned completely black. Like a black hole. You could throw in anything you liked, I wouldn't even notice—my head was drifting through the clouds—everything would just go right in, things just kept going in. And all the while my heart kept its eyes trained on the door. I'd flip through a magazine, but my heart wouldn't be in it at all. My eyes would just skitter nervously across the surface of the page. I began remembering all the bad things I'd discovered about Yoshihiro, making them even worse. And with each moment that passed, that dark side of him kept spreading slowly through all the different parts of my body, until eventually it covered everything. That's how it felt. I was dragging all this black stuff along behind me, it was so heavy I could barely stand—so it was night by the time I headed home. I'd go home and go to sleep waiting for his call, that's what I thought. There had to be some reason. I'll understand if only we can talk about it. That's all I thought."

She talked to me about her heart, how it closed up as she waited.

"Well, shall we head out?" Ken'ichi stood up.

"Yeah. But you know, I have to say that I'm delighted to get this money back. It's like a dream," I said. Ken'ichi told me

49

not to go overboard, and grinned. I tagged along after him, weaving between the couches, walking across the carpet, heading for the door. My eyes were still bouncing around, attempting to locate Sarah. And then I noticed a blond woman standing over by the front desk with her back toward me—I noticed that her back was a lot like Sarah's. As were her clothes, her hairstyle, her height.

I called out to Ken'ichi. "Listen, I just saw someone I know. I'll talk to you later, okay?"

He told me to let him know if I heard any new rumors and walked off.

I drew closer to the woman, my head whirling, trying to get a look at her face. The rug was so thick and soft that it made me feel strange, and my attention was so sharply focused on the woman that I didn't notice what I was doing until I felt something collide with my hip. I stumbled and regained my balance. Then, wondering what on earth had happened, I looked down and saw a small foreign boy who had fallen down and was lying on his back. I took his hands in mine and helped him up.

"Sorry," I said.

As soon as I saw those eyes of his looking back at me, such a commotion broke loose in my chest that it frightened me. His hair was brown, his eyes dark brown. Slowly I readjusted my gaze and went on staring at him.

"This is Sarah's child, my brother's child, absolutely."

Again and again I whispered these words to myself.

I hadn't seen eyes like these anywhere else. The powerful light in them, perfectly at ease—the lips slightly puckered, this expression—the shoulders that reminded you of someone wearing too large a suit . . . seeing him reawakened all the old memories I had, called them forth. I wanted to let Mari know. Before my father, even before my mother—Mari. Finally I managed to gather every bit of strength I had, to mold my lips— it was unlikely that we'd ever meet again, after all—into a smile softer and more gentle than any I'd ever given any lover of mine, and asked the child, "Are you okay?"

He gave me a tiny smile and nodded, and then strode off toward . . .

Sarah.

The woman at the front desk, the person I'd thought was Sarah—I realized now that I'd made a mistake, that I'd had the wrong person. Because the real Sarah, who was standing a little ways off, looked completely different now. But there was no mistake, it was definitely her standing there, the same Sarah I'd met on that day so long ago.

The same Sarah who'd patiently drilled me on the pronunciation of the word "refrigerator." The same Sarah who'd still had a slightly girlish aura about her. The same Sarah who'd been a little weak, a little bit naive.

The Sarah before me now was fitted out in an extremely sharp navy blue suit, and she'd had her hair cut short. She was standing beside a large trunk, her back held perfectly straight, and there was a small blond girl hanging on to her, evidently unwilling to move away. The boy walked over and joined them, started talking pleasantly with the girl. They must be brother and sister. Then all of a sudden a young, sturdily built American man came walking over to them, having settled the bill, apparently sorry to have kept her waiting.

It was then that Sarah noticed me.

First suspiciously, and then suddenly with a look of relief and sorrow, she stared at me with her crystal-clear, sky-blue eyes. She kept blinking, again and again, as if she were trying to make sure it was me. And then it seemed as if she'd lifted the corners of her mouth ever so slightly in a smile.

I understood everything now. Even if Sarah wanted to come to see Mari and me, she couldn't—she couldn't talk to us. But having come to Japan, she'd been unable to refrain from calling. I understood why. I understood the anguish Sarah and that young man had struggled through. And so, after nodding firmly to show that I understood, I turned away. I'm sure the four of them walked out of the hotel not long after, a happy American family. Only Sarah must have kept turning back, looking my way again and again.

I turned around after a while to make sure they were no longer there, and then all the strength slipped from my body and I sank back down into one of the couches. My head was swirling, and my palms were still hot with the touch of that boy's tiny hands. It felt like something was starting to change there, like some transformation was blossoming out from my hands.

The lobby seemed utterly empty now that they were gone . . . it seemed as if nothing at all was left. The sounds of cups clinking together and the clump of people's steps just kept repeating, streaming on and on. That was all.

I arrived back home feeling completely worn out.

The interior of the house was dark and wrapped in silence when I opened the door—evidently my mother was out. I walked straight to the bathroom and slowly washed my face, gazing at the mirror, swearing to it that as long as I lived I would never say a word to anyone about what I'd just seen. And then beyond the edges of my reflection, those features so similar to my brother's—a recollection of those brown eyes. *I've seen him, there's nothing I can do about it now. And we didn't just happen to run into each other, either. I went there intentionally, specifically for that reason.* These thoughts made me feel even more exhausted than I had before.

I decided to change my clothes. On my way to my room, I passed the living room door.

And then I heard her voice.

"Shibami?"

It was quite a surprise. I opened the door and found that, for some reason unknown to me, Mari was lying on our couch, her eyes half open, looking sleepy, just as if she'd been living there all along.

I really had no idea what was going on anymore.

"What are you doing here?" I said.

"You said last night that I ought to come visit during the day, didn't you? So I came, but then . . . there was nobody around, you know, so . . . oh-h-a-a-h!" Mari yawned.

"Why didn't you use the bed in the guest room? Didn't you have trouble falling asleep on the couch?" I asked. She'd been sleeping with her body curled up into a little ball, like a child taking a nap.

"No. It was too bright in the guest ro-o-oh-ohm . . ."

Now that she'd mentioned it, I remembered that we'd sent all the curtains in the guest room to the cleaners. Mari's voice sounded charmed and kind of fuzzy, as if half of her was still dreaming. Her eyes seemed to be focused on something way off in the distance, as people's eyes do when they're feeling tired. Her eyes were beautiful.

"It's gotten cloudy out, you know." I said this with the same feeling I'd have had saying words whose meaning was something extraordinarily tender. I walked over to the window on the other side of the couch where she was lying and opened the curtains. Suddenly the room filled with a hazy brightness.

I looked up at the overcast sky.

"Maybe it'll rain. Or maybe it'll snow," I said.

Just then Mari sprang up into a sitting position, and her expression changed—she drew her eyebrows together and stared at me. Her eyes looked wild, almost demented.

"What? What's wrong?" I asked.

I started feeling extremely uneasy. It even seemed like her

face was mirroring my unease. I hadn't seen her look this strange in ages.

"Let me see something," Mari said.

Then she touched my hands—the hands that boy had touched.

She looked up at me, her face utterly vacant.

"You were with Yoshihiro?"

Her voice was extremely faint, so faint that it took me a while to figure out what she was saying. I shuddered and detached her hands from mine, practically flinging them away.

Finally I managed to speak. "Nope."

My voice was dry, and it was an odd way to answer.

"Of course you weren't, what on earth am I saying? Nobody's going to be seeing him or doing anything with him anymore, are they? I'm still half asleep, I was getting things all mixed up with the dream I'd been having."

Mari pressed her fingers to her temples as she said this.

"My brother died a long time ago," I said.

"I know that," she replied.

She sounded the same as always.

"It's just that I was having this dream. Just before. And there happened to be this scene in it where you'd gotten together with Yoshihiro and the two of you were talking, you know? You were . . . I don't know, it was someplace bright, like a hotel lobby or something."

I didn't know how to reply. So I just said, "Oh."

The instant I spoke I felt something warm pierce my heart.

"Wow, you were right. It's raining!" Mari said

She was looking up out of the window.

The sky was dark. You could feel the rush of the rain, of those large drops of water streaming down, gradually closing over the town. The heavy sky, thickly layered with lead-gray clouds, stretched off into the distance. Would their plane have left the airport by now? Or would they be sitting at the gate, pleasantly chatting of this and that? That family—four people I'd never see again. In the midst of the airport's incessant bustle, the floor around them gleaming beneath the lights, a scene just like the one I entered when I went to see my brother off to America, and when I went to welcome him back. I called the scene up in my mind, as if to make sure that I still remembered.

"Mari, I'm sure this is going to turn to snow tonight. I'll ask my mother to call your house, okay? That way you can stay over tonight."

"Sounds good to me," Mari said.

She went on looking at the rain, her back to me.

I slipped quietly from the room and closed the door.

Since all that money had actually come back, and since this is the kind of thing that almost never happens, I got out my umbrella and set out to spend.

On rainy afternoons, department stores always seem strangely bright and warm, and you can smell the moisture. I headed for the book section and bought nearly a ton of books, and then went and got a few CDs. There were no lines at any of the counters, and it was very quiet, everything neatly arranged. There were just a few shoppers scattered here and there, and the unoccupied clerks all looked extremely elegant.

Even after I'd bought all this I still had some money left over, so after I'd had a cup of tea I went to buy myself a shirt. I found one that I liked a lot, so I was feeling terrifically light-hearted as I started toward the elevator, heading for home . . . then suddenly I found myself passing the sleepwear corner.

Suddenly I remembered. *That's right! Mari's sleeping over tonight!*

I decided to buy her the dark blue, quilted, super-warm-looking pajamas at the very front of the display. They looked so warm and well made that I didn't think there would be any problem even if the wearer suddenly decided to put on a coat and go outside sometime in the middle of the night.

"Is this a present?" asked the clerk.

"Yes, it is," I answered.

The clerk gave the packaged pajamas a red ribbon.

That's it . . . Mari always sleeps in pajamas so thin it makes you shiver just to look at her, and I have that image of her, that's why I wanted to give her these pajamas . . .

Not long after my brother died, Mari ran away from home.

Her parents had been opposed to the relationship from the start, of course, and they'd made her stay home from work for a week without even asking her if she wanted to, using "appendicitis" as an excuse, and they'd even had the nerve to ask that once the week was up she just forget about Yoshihiro—but Mari's running away certainly wasn't in defiance of any of this. She said that she'd just gotten tired. I think this was probably the truth. Her poor parents weren't even a part of her world right then. I was frightened; it terrified me to think that I might be asked to do anything but cry and be with my family, a family now plunged in darkness—and so I didn't see Mari. Even when I heard that she'd run away from home I didn't feel any particular urgency . . . or perhaps I ought to say that I couldn't feel that way, that I didn't have that freedom.

A week had passed since Mari's disappearance when her mother called for the second time, sounding half crazy. For the first time I reacted, decided to see what I could do. I had a feeling I knew where she was.

Spring was drawing near, and that afternoon the sun was warm and the air was heavy with the scent of flowers. I didn't even wear a jacket.

I got on the train.

Mari and Yoshihiro had rented a small one-room apartment in the next neighborhod where they went for their rendezvous. I figured that if Mari was anywhere, she had to be there. *But what will I do if I find her there, dead?* This thought kept circling through my head. Silent spring scenery shook past outside the window, and the faces of the people sitting in their seats looked peaceful and vague. *If I'm too late, if I just find her body, will I feel sorry?* Pale light shot through the swaying interior of the train. *No, as a matter of fact I probably won't, not particularly.* This is what I thought at the time. And I honestly believed it.

I told the people in the maintenance room that I was Yoshihiro's sister and borrowed a key, then rode the slow elevator up to her floor. There was no response when I pressed the doorbell. So I slipped the key into the lock and went inside. The room was dark and unbelievably cold. The blinds were all shut, the air so chilly I felt the cold pushing up through the bottoms of my socks into my feet. I had never been so scared in my life. I walked forward one step at a time, imagining the corpse I was just about to see. Soon my eyes grew accustomed to the dark, and I discovered Mari lying on the floor, wrapped up in a blanket.

She was breathing, inhaling and exhaling slowly, deeply, the way people do when they're asleep. It was a healthy sound, not the sound of someone who's taken sleeping pills. I shook her awake, and she groaned and rubbed her eyes. I was shocked to find myself looking at her bare arms sticking out from the sleeves of a short-sleeve T-shirt. Looking under the blanket I saw that all she was wearing was that T-shirt and a pair of panties. She might as well have been taking an afternoon nap at some resort in the full heat of summer.

"Mari, did you walk here like that?" I asked.

She shook her head and then pointed to the floor. Her coat and a sweater and everything down to her stockings lay scattered around the room.

Mari remained silent and abstracted, almost as if she was in shock.

"Listen, Mari, let's go to my house," I said. "I'll ask my parents to give your mom a call, and then you can just stay in the guest room, you can stay there all by yourself, you don't even have to open the door."

She made no reply. The room was too dark, I couldn't see the expression on her face. But the feeling I got from her was so bitterly cold that it compelled me to hurry. I pushed her arms into the coat, bundled up the rest of her clothes, and led her from the apartment. I hailed a taxi, and we headed for home. Mari turned to look back several times on the way. I had no idea what she was looking at, but I watched her gazing steadily with those cold eyes at the scenery dropping away behind us.

My mother's persuasion and Mari's stubborn insistence that she didn't want to go back home for a while convinced her parents to let her stay. It was arranged that she would stay with us for a while, living in the guest room.

I took care of everything involved in giving up the apartment—that room, of whose existence only my brother and Mari and I had been aware—by myself. There wasn't very much in the way of furniture and decorations and so on, but I found ways to dispose of what there was, and made sure to cancel the lease. It was pretty rough having to do all this in secret, but then there was the deposit: I made up my mind to keep whatever came back as a fee for the work I'd done. Of course they'd rented the place for such a short time and the lease had been canceled so suddenly, and then on top of that my brother had made holes in one of the walls to put up shelves, so in the end I didn't get very much at all.

Yoshihiro was dead, and Mari had settled down in our house, so there was no reason why our parents shouldn't know about the apartment. But if they found out, Mari would be forced to remember the coldness of that room once more, and I hated the idea of letting that happen.

Maybe I was trying to make amends for having thought it wouldn't matter if she died.

I arrived home just in time for dinner.

Mari sat between my mother and father, as if she were their daughter.

"You sure took your time," she said, smiling. "Shall we begin?"

My father, unable to wait, had already started eating. The room was filled with steam, and it was hot, and my mother came and set a pot down on the table, holding it firmly between pot holders, laughing.

"It's Mari's favorite—chicken curry!" she said.

As soon as I'd sat down I passed the large, ribbon-wrapped package over to Mari. "It's a present. I had a bit of a windfall today."

For some entirely obscure reason my father started clapping.

Mari grinned, narrowing her eyes ever so slightly.

"I feel like it's my birthday," she said.

* * *

*T*he rain turned to snow and quietly began to pile up.

Mari said she'd sleep with me in my room, so I suggested that maybe we could go to sleep in the guest room instead, playing video games.

She sat on top of her futon, which was right next to mine, looking warm and cozy in the blue pajamas I'd given her. The room was quite dark, and only the world beyond the window, that world of tumbling snow, looked white. The light from the television flickered down onto our futons. The newscaster was saying that there would be heavy snowfall in Tokyo again overnight.

"It's funny, it didn't snow at all last year," I said.

"Didn't it? I was so completely out of it that I don't remember." Mari smiled. "This sure has been a strange year. Like a dream. I wonder—do you think maybe my condition has improved a bit since last year?"

"It sure looks that way," I said, laughing.

"I mean, what *was* he?" Mari said.

She was talking about my brother.

"I don't think he was actually human. I really don't," I replied, investing these words with as much meaning as possible. Of course he was nothing more than one vibrantly charismatic young man, but since his death was so sudden and meaningless, and because until he died he'd made life as enjoyable as he possibly could, his existence had taken on a peculiar meaning.

"Now, whenever I think about my brother I start feeling really weird, sort of dazzled. I think about how his face looked when he smiled, and of his voice, and of the way his face looked when he was asleep . . . and I start to wonder if he was ever really here, you know, and if he was, it seems like maybe his being here was something irreplaceable—that's how I feel."

"You too?" Mari said.

"And Sarah too, I bet."

"Everyone who knew him."

Was Mari the winner, or Sarah? For a moment I considered this question very seriously. But it was hard to say who had come out ahead. Thanks to Yoshihiro they'd each arrived at places they'd never anticipated.

"During this past year I spent a lot of time wondering how on earth I got to be where I was," Mari said. "It seems like after I fell in love at the airport that day I just noticed that I'd ended up like this, in this place. There was nothing left anywhere around me, there was nothing I could do but keep going—I was deep in the heart of night. Slowly I started to figure out where I could start to rebuild things, but there was nothing there. What sort of creature had Yoshihiro been? But no . . . that didn't mean anything either, there was no meaning. That thought is what made it possible for me to settle down and go to sleep."

I sat gazing into space, thinking back over the scene in the hotel, calling up an image of Sarah as she'd looked when I saw her there, and the face of her son, so familiar and so terribly dear to me that it made me shake. And I remembered Mari during the past year, how she'd been as dark and quiet as a shadow, and myself, never far from her, making my own way through a difficult time.

I got under the covers of my futon.

"Listen, Mari. This has been a strange year for the two of us. It's like we've been living in a space different from the rest of our lives, like we've been moving at a different speed. We've been sealed off—it's been very quiet. I'm sure that if we look back on all this later it'll have its own unique coloring, it'll be a single separate block."

"Yes, I think you're right."

Mari climbed down into her futon too, then pushed her arm up and out so that it extended beyond the base of her downturned chin. She showed me the sleeve of her pajamas.

"It'll be this kind of deep blue," she said. "The kind of color that somehow sucks in your eyes and your ears and all your words—the color of a completely closed-in night."

The snow kept falling, and we lay with our faces turned up toward the TV screen, each trying desperately to win the video games we were playing, and then eventually we both drifted off to sleep.

I awoke with a start. Looking over to my side, I saw that Mari was asleep, her face illuminated by the glow of the television. One hand was still holding the controls for the game, and a good half of her body was lying outside of her covers. She looked as if she'd just suddenly dropped dead, right in the middle of things. Under the quiet music of the game I could hear the sound of her breath.

The expression on her face was bizarre. Her face looked pure and lonely, like the face of someone who's been crying. And it hadn't changed at all since a year ago, or since long before that, when Mari was small.

I pulled the covers up over her and switched off the television. Suddenly the room was completely dark. But of course outside the window the same snow continued to tumble down. The fuzzy pale-bright glimmer of the snow streamed into the room through the gap between the curtains.

"Good night," I whispered, and lay down.

Love Songs

Late at night the trees in my garden seemed to shine.

Awash in light from the street, the quiet glittering green of the leaves and the deep brown of the trunk seemed startlingly vivid.

I'd noticed this for the first time just recently, after I'd started drinking more heavily. Each time I looked out on that scenery with drunken eyes I'd be overwhelmed by the unbelievable purity of those colors, and I'd start feeling as if nothing really mattered, like I wouldn't really care at all even if I were to lose everything I had.

This wasn't resignation, or desperation. It was a much more natural form of acceptance, a feeling that arose from a sweep of emotion that was quiet and cool and crystal-clear.

Every night I fell asleep thinking about these things.

Of course I realized that I was drinking too much and that it would be a good idea for me to start drinking less, and during the daytime I always swore that I'd drink only the tiniest amount that night. But then night would come and the first glass of beer would lead to the next and soon I'd be flying along. I'd start thinking about how well I'd sleep if I just drank a little bit more, and I'd find myself fixing yet another gin and tonic.

As the night deepened I'd start increasing the amount of gin, and the drinks would get stronger. And as I munched my way through a bag of the greatest snack this century has produced—Butter Soy Sauce Popcorn—I'd think, *Damn, I've done it again. . . . Here I am drinking.* I never drank enough to make me feel that I'd done something wrong, but I sometimes got a bit of a shock when I discovered that there was an empty bottle standing on the table in front of me.

It was only after my head started reeling and my body started weaving and I tumbled into bed that I'd hear that soothing voice singing.

At first I thought it was my pillow. Because it seemed to me that the pillow that always cradled my cheek so gently—no matter what was happening, however bad things were—would have a voice just like the one I was hearing, just that clear. I only heard the voice when my eyes were closed, so I figured it was a comfy sort of dream. At times like these I was never lucid enough to think very deeply about anything.

The reverberations of that voice wandered sweetly, softly, working like a massage on the area of my heart that was the most tightly clenched, helping those knots to loosen. It was like the rush of waves, and like the laughter of people I'd met in all kinds of places, people I'd become friendly with and then separated from, and like the kind words all those people had said to me, and like the mewing of a cat I had lost, and like the mixture of noises that rang in the background in a place that was dear to me, a place far away, a place that no longer existed, and like the rushing of trees that whisked past my ears as I breathed in the scent of fresh greenery on a trip someplace . . . the voice was like a combination of all this.

That night I heard it again.

A faint song that felt more sensual than an angel's, and also more real. I tried to catch the melody, fixed the little that remained of my consciousness on it, listened desperately. Sleep trickled down around me, and the happy tune dissolved away into my dreams.

Long ago I'd fallen in love with a strange man and ended up acting out one of the parts in a bizarre triangular relationship. He'd been a friend of the guy I was going out with now, and he'd had the aura of a man whom women love fleetingly but with explosive force. Actually, he was a slightly peculiar and rather boisterous sort of guy, something of a thug, I could see that now, but I'd been young at the time and of course I'd fallen for him. I didn't remember much about him anymore. We'd slept together any number of times, done it again and again, but we'd never gone out on the sort of dates where you get to spend time looking at each other, so I could hardly even remember his face.

For some reason I remembered only the nasty woman, Haru.

Apparently Haru and I had both fallen for the man at the same time. As time passed and the two of us kept running into each other at his house, we began little by little to get acquainted, and then toward the end things got so bad that it was almost as if the three of us were living together. Haru was three years older than me, and she worked part-time. I was in college.

Naturally we despised each other, cursed each other, and sometimes we'd even whip out our fists and get tangled up in all-out fights. Never in my life had I come so vividly close to another person, and never in my life had I resented anyone so much. Haru was all that stood in my way. I must have wished for her death a hundred times, and wished in earnest. Of course Haru probably wished for my death too.

Our two loves finally came to an abrupt end one day when the man, exhausted by the life we'd been living, ran off to some faraway place and didn't come back. My relationship with Haru ended then too. I went on living in the same town, but from what I'd heard through the grapevine, Haru had run off to Paris or someplace like that.

That was the last I'd heard of her.

I had no idea why all of a sudden I'd started remembering her, thinking of her almost fondly. I didn't particularly want to see her again, and I wasn't interested in knowing what she was doing. That period in my life had been so filled with passionate emotion that it had ended up spinning around and becoming nothing but a string of blank memories. Ultimately it hadn't made any profound impression on me at all.

Knowing her, it seemed likely that she'd have ended up as some kind of two-bit hustler, sponging off some artist in Paris, or maybe if she was lucky she'd have found some elderly patron and she'd be living off of him, very elegantly. That's the sort of woman she was. She was skinny as a bone, and her manner of talking was irritatingly frigid; her voice was deep, and she always wore black. She had thin lips, and there were always wrinkles carved into the space between her eyebrows, and she complained constantly. Yet when she smiled, she looked sort of like a child.

It kind of hurt to remember her smile.

Of course when you go to sleep having drunk as much as I had, waking up is total hell. It felt like the alcohol had pounded me flat, like my entire body—both inside and out—had been soaking in a bath of hot sake. My mouth was like a desert, and it was a while before I could even roll over.

I couldn't even begin to consider getting up and brushing my teeth, or taking a shower. I found it impossible to believe that in the past I'd done those things quite casually, as if they were nothing at all.

Arrowlike rays of sun bit into my head.

I couldn't even stand to tally up all my symptoms, there were so many, and it was all so terrible that I just wanted to burst into tears. I didn't see how I could ever be saved.

Lately every morning was like this.

Finally I gave up and dragged myself limply out of bed. If I just left my aching head on its own it would start swaying from side to side, so I held it in my hands. Still holding it, I fixed myself a cup of tea and drank it.

For some reason my nights tended to stretch out to surprising lengths, like rubber, and they were endlessly sweet. And my mornings were unforgivingly sharp. The light seemed to stab at me with some sort of pointy object. It was hard and translucent and stubborn. It was wretched.

Every thought I had just made me unhappy. And then, like an army in pursuit of an already thoroughly pummeled foe, the phone started to shriek. It was an awful sound. The insistent clangor got on my nerves so much that I answered with intentionally exaggerated vitality.

"Hello!"

"Wow, you sure sound lively," said Mizuo cheerfully.

Mizuo was my boyfriend. He'd known both Haru and the man. When the two of them made their exits, he and I were left alone.

"I'm not. I've got a hangover and my head's throbbing."

"Not again?"

"You're off today, right? Are you coming over?"

"Yeah, I'll be over soon," Mizuo said.

He hung up.

He owned a store that sold various little household goods, so weekdays were his days off. I'd been working in the same kind of store until recently, but the place had gone out of business. It had been decided that I'd go to work at a new branch Mizuo was about to open in the next town, and

I was waiting for it to open; which would be in about six months.

Every once in a while Mizuo looked at me with the same eyes he used to look at objects. Like he was thinking, *It'd really be better without this floral pattern here . . . it might get a good price if it didn't have this chip . . . this stripe here might look tacky but it captures people's hearts.*

At times like these the look in his eyes was so coldly penetrating it was shocking, and when I noticed it I'd give a little gasp. But it seemed he was also inspecting the changes that took place within my heart, regarding even those as just another pattern.

*H*e brought flowers that afternoon.

We ate sandwiches and a salad, feeling peaceful. I was still stretched out in bed, and every time we kissed he'd chuckle and say things like, "You stink so terribly of alcohol it's amazing. I wouldn't be surprised if your hangover made its way through your mucus membranes into me!" It seemed as if his smile ought to give off a perfume like a flower—maybe something along the lines of a white lily.

Winter was almost over. Though inside the room everything felt incredibly happy, I had the feeling that outside the window things were frighteningly dry. It seemed like the wind blowing past was hitting up against the sky, scraping noisily across its surface.

I figured it was just too sweet inside, too warm.

"I just remembered something," I said. The sweetness and the warmth had reminded me. "I've been having something like a dream every night as I'm about to fall asleep, you know, it's always the same, and so I'm kind of worried that I might be starting to have hallucinations. Except hallucinations aren't supposed to feel very good, are they? Do you think with the amount I'm drinking I could be an alcoholic? Could I be that far gone?"

"Don't be ridiculous," Mizuo said. "Even if you do have something of a tendency toward dependence, the real problem is just that you have time on your hands, so you end up drinking too much—that's all. Things will go back to normal as soon as you start working again, and of course it's totally fine for you to be living the sort of slowed-down life you're living now. But the dream you mentioned . . . what sort of dream is it?"

"I'm not sure I'd actually call it a dream." The pain and the nausea I'd felt were finally starting to soften. In this new mood I tried desperately to trace my way back to that happiness. "It's like . . . I get drunk and tumble into bed, right? And then I start to feel like I'm being sucked up into something, you know, it's like I'm walking in this place that used to be really important to me, a place that's precious to me, but with my eyes closed—that's the sort of feeling I have. There's this nice smell, and I feel so safe and relaxed, and then I start to hear this song, always the same song, ever so faintly. The voice singing it is so sweet I almost start to cry . . . maybe it's not even a song. But it's something like a melody, and it's ever so faint, and it's far away, and it's singing of absolutely perfect joy. Yeah, and it's always the same melody."

"Sounds bad. You must be an alcoholic."

"Huh?" I squinted at him, startled.

Mizuo burst out laughing. "Just kidding. Actually I've heard a story like that before. In fact it was just like yours. They say it means someone wants to speak to you."

"What do you mean someone? Who?"

"Someone who's died. Has anyone you know died?"

I puzzled for a bit, but no one came to mind. I shook my head.

"They say that when a dead person wants to say something to someone it was close to in life, that's how it gets the message across. And when you get drunk or when you're just about to fall asleep, at times like that it's easier to get synchronized, you know, so that's when it happens. Anyway that's what I heard somewhere."

Suddenly I felt icy cold. I pulled the blanket up over my shoulders.

"Is it always someone you know?" I asked.

No matter how happy the song made me feel, the idea of having some dead stranger singing into my ear was not something I liked.

"So they say. Maybe . . . could it be Haru?" he said.

Mizuo is very quick to sense these things. And it's true—I gave a little start and felt almost immediately that he was probably right. In fact what I felt was almost a certainty. I hadn't heard a word from her, and then lately all these memories of her drifting through my mind. . . .

"You should see what you can find out."

"Yeah, I'll ask some friends," I said.

Mizuo nodded.

No matter what people said to him, Mizuo never butted in with stories of his own or ignored what they were saying. His parents must have raised him well. And yet you can't deny that his name—Mizuo, written with characters meaning "water" and "man"—is fairly weird, and it's certainly not easy to try and figure out how his parents came up with it. The extraordinary truth is that when his mother was young, conditions made it necessary for her to have an abortion, even though she didn't want one. When she had Mizuo she named him "waterman," hoping that he'd be happy enough for two—the fetus that had been lost, the "waterbaby" as they're called in Japanese, and himself.

Is that the sort of name you give a child?

The whole interior of the room was flooded with the sweet scent of the white roses he'd brought. It occurred to me that if the scent lasted until night, I might be able to fall asleep without drinking so much. We kissed once again and embraced.

★ ★ ★

"Yeah, Haru died."

This half-expected answer came so smoothly it was shocking.

Mizuo had told me that a guy whom Haru and the man and I had all known was working at a certain all-night coffee shop now, and so I'd jumped in a taxi and rushed straight there, hoping he might be able to tell me something—I'd made a special trip, in fact—and this was the answer I got. If that was all he was going to say, I might as well just have called. I spent a few moments peering at his eyes and understood that he wasn't joking. He was standing behind the crowded shop's counter, dressed in his waiter's uniform, drying dishes. His eyes were grim.

"You mean overseas? How? Did she have AIDS?" I asked.

"It was drinking. She died from drinking," he said quietly.

Icy chills, like a double shock, jittered down my spine. For an instant I felt sure I must be cursed, just as she'd been.

"She got to where she was drunk all the time, and then one day in the apartment her patron kept for her she just . . . she'd been in and out of some specialist rehab center for alcoholics, and from what I hear it sounds like she just totally collapsed toward the end. This friend of mine who just got back from Paris told me about it—said he'd heard it all from some guy who was close to her."

"Oh."

I took a gulp of coffee and nodded slightly, as if appreciating the flavor.

BANANA YOSHIMOTO

"I thought you two hated each other's guts. What's up?"

"'Even travelers who brush sleeves on the road are bound by ties from a former life'... isn't exactly what I mean, but I hadn't heard a word from her since she left, you know, so I started wondering what she was doing. After all, I'm with Mizuo now, and I'm happy—you know what I mean?"

"Yeah, stuff like that happens sometimes, doesn't it?"

Back during the days when Haru and the man and I were pretty much living together, this guy was working as a bartender, and I was always going to the bar where he worked, to get drunk and blow off steam. He'd always been completely indifferent to things that were happening in other people's lives, so it was easy to talk to him, and you could talk to him about anything. I sat looking at him now, his form hovering in the dim light of the shop, feeling paralyzed, and found myself remembering the feeling that had hung in the air in those days—felt it all coming back. Weary, tomorrowless, smoldering. I certainly had no desire to put myself back there, to feel the sensations whose memory I was now reliving, and yet they called up an odd sentimentality.

"Well, so Haru's no longer in this world," I said.

Across the counter my old friend nodded.

I went back to my apartment and drank all alone in memory of Haru. For some reason I felt that it was okay for me to drink a lot that night, so I was able to pour in as much as I wanted and still feel good. In the past, whenever my mind had begun

80

to circle vaguely around thoughts of Haru, an image of the Eiffel Tower had drifted up before me, like a shot of it on television, but tonight the image didn't appear. Instead I saw the world that had opened up inside Haru after she lost the only outlet she'd had for her overabundance of energy, and quickly lost herself in drink. I completely understood what Haru had gone through when the man left, and why she hadn't been able to pull herself together and move on again. Because that's how totally involved our love for him was—both of us had given it everything we could. The man was extremely attractive to begin with, of course, but to tell the truth, Haru and I couldn't have put so much effort into that love if we hadn't been competing. I don't know if he found all this amusing or if it made him feel like he needed some space to breathe or what, but for some reason the man always used to do stuff like invite one of us over to his house and then go out on a date with the other. Toward the end he frequently left Haru and me at his house together and didn't come back all night.

I'm naturally clumsy, and it takes everything I have just to cook a meal or mend some little tear in a piece of clothing, to tie the strings on little packages or put together a cardboard box. Haru was particularly good at that kind of thing, so whenever she found me struggling over something she'd shout out, "God, are you clumsy!" and "I sure would love to see what kind of parents you've got!" and all sorts of stuff, jeering at me without mercy. In return I'd coolly point out that she had no breasts, and that her taste in clothes was absolutely atrocious.

The man was the sort of person who praised what was good and told you honestly that what was bad was bad, and that just spurred the two of us on, making us even more paranoid.

"You really are a foul cook, aren't you? It's unbelievable! It's not as if you're using a microwave. Ugghh, this looks repulsive!" Haru said.

I was making Chinese-style mixed vegetables that night. The man had gone out with her that afternoon, keeping it a secret from me, so I was in no mood to put up with her.

"There's no reason why I should have to listen to such rude things from someone dressed in clothes as laughable as yours. I think you need to have slightly larger breasts to wear black knitwear like that."

Haru jabbed me very sharply in the back with her elbow. I was sautéing vegetables, and my hand very nearly went into the wok.

"What the hell are you doing?" I shouted.

The fierce sizzling of the vegetables and the waves of heat washed over my voice and made it sound achingly sad.

"You have no right to say that," Haru said.

"Maybe not," I replied, and turned off the heat.

Now that the room was suddenly quiet, our silence drifted up into the foreground. By that point neither of us could figure out whether it was okay for us to be sharing the body of a single man—a slightly eccentric man, a man who seemed to be laughing at the world, living life in his own way—and whether it was normal or abnormal. The same was true of the fact that even though he never demanded that we stay, we were spending all our time cooped up in his house, and of the fact that the two of us were always there together. All I knew was that Haru's gloomy voice and her crazy thinness were getting on my nerves. She was always weaving around in front of me, making me want to wring her neck like a chicken's.

"Why are we doing this?" Haru said then, her tone peculiarly absent. "There are other women who like him, you know, but you and I are the only ones doing this stuff. And he's not even here."

"That's how it goes."

"I feel like I'm going crazy, you get on my nerves so much."

"Those ought to be my lines. Anyway, it's too late to complain now."

I found Haru's hackneyed way of thinking about things and her darkly cheerless point of view sickening. I hated it.

"What's with you, anyway? Do you even really want him?" Haru said this as if she were scolding me.

"Yes, I want him!" I said. "That's why I'm stuck here with you, isn't it? With a moron like you—"

Wham!

Apparently I'd said too much. Before I'd even finished speaking Haru slapped me across the cheek with the flat of her hand, producing a loud smack. I was stunned for a moment, unable to grasp what had happened. Then, as the seconds passed, I felt my right cheek getting hotter.

"You've really pissed me off now, so I'm leaving," I said, and stood up. "You can have him tonight. If he comes back."

Haru went on staring at me as I picked up my bag, and then as I walked out the front door. She had her eyes open so wide, and they shone with such an earnest light, that I seriously thought she might call out for me to stop. That's the kind of gleam she had in her eyes. A look that says *Don't go,* not a look that says *I'm sorry.* I suspect that she only remained silent because it would have seemed weird if she'd actually spoken those words.

Her small, fair, tackily made-up face was half hidden by her long hair. I noticed how lovely and insubstantial she looked when you saw her from a distance. Without saying a word I closed the door.

Just thinking about other women I knew sleeping with the man gave me heartburn and left me fuming, and yet where Haru was concerned I no longer minded. In fact there were times, when the three of us were all sleeping together, when he and Haru would start going at it, and I hardly gave it a second thought. If it had been any other woman I probably would have killed her on the spot.

As long as we were together I could sort of understand how the man felt toward her.

I'm not talking about who she was inside.

Inside she was probably just a strange, high-strung, un-pleasant woman. But there was something truly special in her appearance. The soft shadow you saw in her panties, slender shoulders flickering in and out of the blackness of her long hair, odd little valleys over her collarbone, the curves under her breasts that seemed so impossibly, untouchably distant . . . she could have been the embodiment of the diaphanous image, of Woman herself, come shakily to life, stumbling around. That's certainly what you felt.

I saw the glimmering uproar of the trees in my garden again that night, outside the window. It was a beautiful scene, one that seemed to break off in bizarre angles, coming to points, just as I'd remembered. In the wash of light I had the feeling that these points were gentle, not pitilessly hard.

No doubt this was because I was drunk.

I turned out the lights. The various objects in the room were even more sharply visible now.

I could hear my breath, and my heartbeat.

I pulled the covers up over myself and sank my head deep down into the pillow. And then I heard it again.

The reverberations of a voice as pure as an angel's, the light tenderness, the melody—all this made my heart begin to flutter, to dance achingly. Like waves, distant and close, full of nostalgia, rolling on. . . .

Haru, is there something you want to say?

My heart felt like it was spinning, like something that goes on spinning even when it's hidden from view—I tried to lock the spinning on that sound. But there was no sign of Haru, nothing at all but the beautiful stream of sound stabbing through my chest. Perhaps on the other side of this beautiful melody I'd find Haru's smile. Or maybe—maybe she was screaming in a voice filled with hatred that my happiness and her death were two sides of a single sheet of paper. I didn't care, either way I wanted terribly to hear.

I needed to know what she was trying to say. I concentrated so intensely that the space between my eyebrows started to ache, and before long exhaustion rolled out on waves of sleep from the far side of the song. Deep down inside I gave up, murmured words expressing my decision to give up. As if they were the words of a prayer.

I feel bad, Haru. But I can't hear you. I'm sorry.

Good night.

"You were right, Haru's dead," I said.

Mizuo just opened his eyes a little wider; that was it.

"So she really is?" he said, and shifted his gaze to the window.

The glittering nighttime town was stunning.

We were only fourteen stories up, but the view was quite good. I'd suggested that we go eat someplace sky-high for a change, and Mizuo had asked if I meant sky-high in cost or elevation. I'd laughed and said I meant both, and that's how we'd ended up here.

The world beyond the window was awash with shining beads of night, these beads were everywhere—I was overwhelmed. The lines of cars were a necklace circling the rim of night.

"What makes you think it's Haru?" I asked.

"The two of you were so close to each other."

He said this in a perfectly ordinary tone, then cut himself a bit of meat and lifted it to his mouth. For a moment my hands stopped moving. Because all of a sudden I was on the verge of tears.

"Does Haru want to say something to me?"

"Afraid I wouldn't know that."

"No, I guess not."

I looked back down at my dinner. Maybe it wasn't such a big deal after all. Maybe the various lingering regrets that kept drifting up to the surface now that my alcohol-spattered life was getting ready to enter a new stage had simply taken form as an image of Haru. We'd already emptied two bottles of wine tonight—I'd had help from Mizuo—and the world before me was starting to get fuzzy around the edges.

I felt like I wouldn't mind even if those inescapable regrets that we're all left with, that lie buried deep inside every one of us, ended up being nothing more than a bit of color added to the night—as long as I could enjoy the incredible beauty of this quietly blurring, infinitely reflected scenery until morning, when everything would return once again to zero.

"Would you like to go see Haru now?" Mizuo asked suddenly.

"Excuse me?" I said this in a rather jarring tone. I was so taken aback that the other people in the restaurant glanced over at me.

"I know a guy who can do that sort of stuff," Mizuo said, grinning.

"This sounds extre-e-emely suspect," I replied, and grinned back.

"Actually, it's pretty impressive. The guy's a midget—I got to know him way back when I was doing a kind of work much more unsavory than what I'm doing now. He lets you talk to dead people. It's kind of like hypnotism, you know, except it's totally real," Mizuo said.

"And you've tried this?" I asked.

"Yeah. I once killed someone, see, by mistake."

These words just slipped off his tongue. His casualness indicated how unfathomably deep his remorse was.

"What, in a fight or something?"

"Nope. I lent him my car when it was broken."

Mizuo seemed unwilling to say more. He changed the topic. "It left a really bad aftertaste, you know, so I went to this midget . . . and then I met the guy and talked things over with him, and even if it was bogus it made me feel better—it totally cleared the air. And I meant it when I said that I think you and Haru were close to each other. If there hadn't been a man standing between you, I'm sure you would have hit it off really well. That guy has turned into a real loser now, and he's living a sleazy life, but back then he had this super-cheery kind of air about him, right? I always thought that since the two of you reacted in the same way to that sort of radiance, you must be pretty similar."

It occurred to me once again that the coldness of Mizuo's personality was like that of water, just as his name suggested. I realized that the trees and all kinds of other things scattered throughout the gorgeous scene spread beneath the window— a scene that ought to have been perfectly still—were shaking. There must be a strong wind blowing. The headlights of cars kept flowing on, quietly burying the streets.

"Of course you're much more my type. Flat nose, klutzy . . ."

He said this in the same tone he'd use to say that a chipped vase had a certain appeal, and I liked that way of speaking, so I thought again how much I liked Mizuo.

"Okay, let's go see the midget," I said. "It sounds neat."

"You bet it is," Mizuo replied, sipping his wine. "Even if it's a lie, even if it's who knows what, if it clears the air, you know, if it's fun, you might as well try it. As long as it makes you feel better, it's all right."

★ ★ ★

*T*he shop Mizuo took me to was an ordinary snack bar, the sort of place you come across all over, down below street level, with nothing in it but a counter. There was no denying that the man in charge was a midget. But apart from the badly proportioned arrangement of his body, he seemed like a regular enough person, and there was nothing about him that made you feel uncomfortable. He gazed at me with steady eyes.

"Your girlfriend?" the midget asked Mizuo suddenly.

"Yeah—her name's Fumi."

I nodded slightly and said it was nice to meet him.

"This here's my buddy, Tanaka the midget."

Tanaka laughed when Mizuo said this.

"If I were an American I'd be Mr. John Doe," he said. "That's me."

He was about as sketchy as you can get, but the intelligence behind his words made me feel that I could trust him. He pushed open the small gate and stepped out from behind the counter, then walked over to the heavy front door and turned the lock.

"You're here to see someone dead?" he said.

"Right. Got to keep you working!" Mizuo said, grinning.

"I haven't been doing this at all lately. Takes strength. I have to charge a lot," Tanaka said, and looked at me. "When did this person die?"

"Just recently. She's a young woman—I hadn't seen her in about two years. We were battling each other over a man."

My heart was pounding fast and hard. "I wonder if I could have something to drink?"

"Yeah, I could use something too. Break out a bottle," Mizuo said.

"Well then, tonight the bar is yours," Tanaka said.

He climbed a ladder and took a bottle down from one of the shelves up near the top, then started mixing two whiskeys and soda, moving his hands quickly and deftly.

"This one here's been overdoing it lately," Mizuo said, with a smile. "You better make it super strong."

"Gotcha."

Tanaka laughed, and I laughed along with him. There was something I kept noticing. Mizuo trusted me, he treated me just like he would any adult. And that called forth an incomparable feeling of relief and security. I really believe that no matter how old people get, they tend to change in certain ways depending on how people treat them—they change their colors. Mizuo was always very skilled at using people. We said cheers and drank.

"*I* don't get it," said Tanaka, tilting his head slightly to the side. "Why would you want to see a woman you fought with over a man?"

My mouth felt numb from the strong whiskey and soda.

I answered him honestly. "It seems we may really have liked each other. In fact we might have had a little lesbian dynamic going on."

Tanaka exploded into laughter. "You're honest, good for you."

I kept gazing vaguely at his small shoes, inspecting the shape of his tiny hands, thinking about what I'd say to Haru if I actually connected with her. But as hard as I tried, I couldn't think of anything.

"Shall we start?" Tanaka said. We'd finished our drinks.

Mizuo had become very quiet. No doubt he was thinking of the things that had happened when he'd come here himself, long ago.

"What do you mean? How do we start?" I asked.

"It's simple. You don't have to take any drugs, and there's no counting involved. All you've got to do is close your eyes and keep quiet and you'll go to this room. That's the room where the meetings take place. There's just one thing I ought to warn you about, and that's that even if she invites you to leave, you can't step outside that door. You remember what happened to Earless Hôichi in the old ghost story when he went along with the ghost. That's how he became earless. And there have been plenty of people like that—people who leave the room and then realize that they can't get back. A few of them never returned. So you've got to be careful, see?"

I was now so scared I couldn't even speak.

Mizuo saw this and laughed. "Don't worry, you'll be fine," he said. "You're strong."

I nodded and closed my eyes. I sensed that Tanaka had come out from behind the counter again. Almost immediately I felt a smooth coolness spread quietly through my body.

Suddenly I found myself in the room.

It was a strange, cramped room, with one small frosted glass window. I was sitting on a worn red sofa. There was a second small sofa shaped just like mine directly across from me—there wasn't even a table in the middle. It was a lot like the House of Surprises that they used to have way back when, in amusement parks, that thing where the walls rotate, and even though you're not moving you have the illusion that the whole house is spinning. The lights were dim, and I felt sort of melancholy.

And then there was the wooden door.

I figured it would probably be okay if I just touched it, so I stretched my hand out toward the doorknob. It was narrow and soothingly cool, a dull gold in color. The moment I closed my hand around it, I felt a sweep of vibrations come throbbing up into my arm. If I had to describe the feeling, I'd say it was as if the door were holding something back, as if this were the only quiet place in an incredible whirl of energy that was spiraling around outside, someplace like the eye of a hurricane, or like walled-off sacred ground. Every cell in my body started to quake and gibber. I realized that I had an instinctive fear of the world beyond that door.

Yet at the same time I could understand that certain people might be tempted to open this door. I understood that Mizuo

93

must have felt that urge. And that several people had stepped outside, and that it was true—those people had probably never come back.

Yeah, it makes sense.

I stepped away from the door and sat back down on the couch. My head had cleared. I stamped my feet on the wooden floor and slid my hands across the sandpapery beige wall. Everything felt extremely real. Like the deserted waiting room of a train station way out in the country, the room had a certain unnatural feeling about it, a certain oppressive air.

And then it happened. All of a sudden the door crashed open and Haru came bounding into the room.

I was so surprised I couldn't speak.

For just a moment, over the top of Haru's shoulders, I caught a glimpse of a tremendous expanse of heavy ash-colored gray, and heard a wild moaning, like the noise of some kind of storm. That scenery was any number of times more frightening for me than the fact that Haru had actually come.

"It's been a while," Haru said.

She gave me a small smile, tightening her lips.

You had the feeling that smile would be sucked up by the room and by the frightening grayness outside almost before you knew it. It seemed like a terribly lonely smile.

"It's great that we're able to meet like this," I said.

The words came out as smooth as oil.

"I'm glad I figured out that you wanted to see me. Because to tell the truth, I liked you a lot, Haru, you know? The days we spent together had this special feeling of tension—it was a lot of fun. And that's only because it was you. You mean a lot to me. And just being with you taught me so much. There were all these things that I wanted to talk to you about, but we never had the chance. I really regret that."

I couldn't say that this was all the truth. It was like a confession. It was like shouting love at a boat as it glides off into the distance.

But Haru—thin as ever, still dressed in black—nodded.

"Me too," she said. Then, "But take a look at this!"

She stood up. And as she did, a bit of her long hair brushed lightly across my hand. It was an amazingly swishy, ticklish feeling.

I focused on the sensation to make sure it was real.

It was then that she yanked the door open.

I stiffened, readying myself.

Even if she invites you to leave, you can't step outside.

Haru giggled, gently brushing aside my ungenerous impulses. "Boy, are you suspicious! It's okay, I'm just showing you. Here, watch this, I'll put my head out. Okay?"

Haru thrust her head back into that ash-gray world. And the instant she did so her hair began to flap and tangle with awesome energy, but without making any sound at all. She kept her head thrust back as she spoke.

"You remember that day when there was a huge storm like this and you and I were in his house alone? It felt just like it does here. You know, I made my way through this storm

95

with my eyes shut, that's how I got here. I did that because I wanted to see you. I mean, I wouldn't have come for that man we were both so crazy about, you know, seriously. Because it's rough getting here, it really is rough."

"Same for me," I said. "It seemed like I should see you."

"Because I was calling you, kiddo. I'd been hanging around for a while, you know, down where you were," Haru said.

She seemed much more grown up than the Haru I'd known.

"Why did you call me?" I asked.

"I don't really know. Maybe because I never felt lonely when we were together. I mean I wasn't ever truly lonely, but whenever I think about you I get this feeling that I was least lonely when I was with you. And I get the feeling that on the day of that storm, you know, I wanted to kiss you."

There was no expression on Haru's face.

"I'm happy to hear that," I said.

But I felt unbearably sad. The ash gray outside was so heavy that I felt how great a distance separates us from the past when I looked at Haru's tangled hair whipping in the wind. It was a distance greater than that between life and death, wider than the unfillable chasm that separates us all from one another.

I called her name. "Haru!"

Haru gave a little smile and fixed her hair, took hold of the door with a movement that seemed perfectly natural, said good-bye and touched my hand, then vanished into the space beyond the door. I was thinking: *Yeah, come to think of it, I guess the only time we ever talked to each other like this was that day, that was the only time. . . .*

The bang of the door and the coldness of her hand lingered on.

"*W*elcome back!" shouted Tanaka.

Glancing quickly around, I realized that I was back in the shop.

"Wow! That was awesome! What's the trick?" I said.

I was trying to hide my confusion, but I was also genuinely impressed.

"That's a nice thing to say! It's the real thing, kid." Tanaka sounded slightly pissed off.

"Basically, Tanaka here is like that animal the Chinese thought up that eats people's bad dreams, see? Think of it that way," Mizuo said.

"Right, that's a good way to put it," Tanaka said.

"Yeah, I guess so. It made me really happy to see her. I don't know, it's like some poison has been sucked out of my chest," I said.

I felt myself gradually returning to reality—I checked to make sure that my mind and body were still as they should be. My breath, and everything I saw, was so sharp and clear it seemed like some mist dissolving.

"You feel like you do after you get a lot of exercise, right?" Tanaka said, plonking a glass of ice water down on the counter in front of me. "That's because you've just been someplace very far away."

*Y*es—that stormy day.

Early autumn and a typhoon had blown up.

The situation between Haru and me had been steadily getting more and more dangerous, and we'd been quarreling the entire week. Our love for the man was starting to wear thin, and there was nothing we could do to turn things around, so we were constantly irritated and always anxious. The man almost never came by the house anymore, but neither of us cared much about that.

"It's thundering like crazy outside," I said.

I wanted to go home but I couldn't go home, so I had no choice but to say something to Haru; I'd unthinkingly made the mistake of speaking. But she responded in a surprisingly ordinary tone.

"I wish it would stop. I hate thunder."

She drew her eyebrows together. It was an extremely erotic, sorrowful expression, and every time I saw it I felt charmed—if only for an instant.

"Fumi! Help me, I'm scared!"

There'd been a bright flash of lightning, and then almost immediately a growl of thunder so fierce it was like getting hit on the head. It was the first time Haru had ever said anything like that to me, and so I looked over at her, stunned, and found that she was sitting facing me, grinning like a little girl. Suddenly I understood. *Haru knows too. This love affair is moving through its final stage, and after that the two of us will never see each other again. She knows it as well as I do.*

"It's pretty close," I said.

"I really wish it'd stop," Haru repeated.

She moved away from the window and circled around behind my back, pretending that she was trying to hide.

No doubt the coming of the storm had made her feel lonely.

"Don't give me that. You're not scared," I said, my voice incredulous. I turned around to look at her.

"Actually, I am a little scared."

Haru laughed. I smiled back.

And then her face filled with surprise.

"Hey, aren't we kind of getting along? Just a bit?"

I nodded. "You know, I think maybe we are."

The room was shut off from the rest of the world, and the thunder kept crashing over us, again and again, coming from ever so far away. The air that filled the room had turned thick and hard, and it felt as if even our silenced breathing was disturbing that small perfection. Nothing but a certain sense of preciousness glittered there, steeped in stillness and quiet. Soon it would all be over. All of this would wither away, it would all disappear. We'd go our separate ways. Again and again this conviction crashed over us.

"I wonder how he's doing in all this."

Haru's profile looked small and beautiful in the flashes of light.

"It certainly is stormy out."

I wanted us to be still now. Together, quiet and still.

"Do you think he's got an umbrella?"

"It wouldn't help in this weather. You'd get hit by lightning."

"It'd suit him, wouldn't it? A death like that."

"I wish he'd hurry up and come home."

"Yeah."

We sat alongside each other, leaning up against the wall, hugging our knees and talking. This was the only time I ever spoke with Haru like that—it had never happened before and it would never happen again. The flowing roar of the rain never stopped getting in the way of our thoughts. It felt like the whole time we'd been in this room we'd been friends, as close to each other as we were right now. Like all along we'd just been pretending not to like each other.

"It sounds like a flash flood."

"Yeah. It hasn't rained like this in a while."

"I wonder where he could be."

"Anywhere's okay as long as he's safe."

"Don't worry, he's fine."

"Yeah, he's probably fine."

Haru was hugging her knees, resting her narrow chin on her kneecaps.

She nodded elegantly and strongly.

★ ★ ★

*I*t was close to dawn when Mizuo and I left Tanaka's shop.

I questioned him as we walked. "So how long was I actually unconscious?"

"About two hours. We drank as we waited—and boy, am I drunk!"

Mizuo's voice echoed loudly in the deserted alley.

"Really? Was it that long?"

I'd only been with Haru for a few moments, so I was surprised to hear this. All the same, I was feeling cool and relaxed. The light of the moon and stars was incredibly vivid, so brilliant it seemed as if they'd been washed, and it felt like I hadn't seen them so bright in years. It made me feel happy just to walk, and my pace sped up all on its own. *Haru, an angel's song, the midget medium, Haru. . . .*

"But that's fine. As long as you feel better," Mizuo said suddenly, and then put his arm around my shoulder. "For now, don't think."

I nodded without saying anything.

Did I just happen to get drunk every night?

Was Haru always somewhere close by?

Was that beautiful song Haru trying to call me?

Where did I go just now at the shop?

Who was that midget? Why is he able to do that?

Was that really Haru? Even though she's dead?

Or was it just a one-person play acted out inside me?

And then Haru made her exit, and I was left alone.

Greater than all the mysteries, a calm evening breeze slid through me, cleansing me.

"I kind of feel like, starting tomorrow, I won't be drinking that much. I wonder if I've been doing it on purpose," I said. "But I don't know . . . it really seems like I'll be able to stop."

"I'm sure you've just reached that stage." Mizuo smiled.

Is everything just a "stage" for Mizuo? All these things inside me, and his being with me?

Isn't he excessively gentle because he's excessively cold?

I have no idea what's coming, and if I love him any more than I do now, I'll probably become completely transparent.

What will happen to us as we begin our new life together?

And yet . . .

Mizuo's smile still seemed to pierce straight through to my heart, and I had the feeling that this smile was the spitting image of the cold and beautiful night. Even if this night we were spending together and everything else was just going to disappear into the past, that was all right—and it seemed to me that I held this allrightness preciously in my hands, and that it was glittering there. Just like the time I'd spent with Haru.

At any rate, I'd probably never hear that singing voice again, that voice so lovely it made you shudder: suddenly I understood this. And that alone made me feel terribly sad.

That feeling of security, that sweetness, that pain, that gentleness. I felt sure that every time I saw the green of the trees in my garden awash in light from the street, I'd be struck by a sudden flicker of remembrance—the tail of that soft melody—and I'd chase along behind it, as if sniffing my way forward in pursuit of a pleasant scent.

And then I'd stop wanting to remember, and I'd forget.

Walking with Mizuo's hand on my shoulder, I realized this.

Asleep

*W*hen did I start sleeping so much whenever I was alone? Sleep would rush over me like an incoming tide. There was nothing I could do to resist it. And this sleep was infinitely deep, so deep that neither the ringing of the phone nor the rumble of the cars driving by outside found their way to my ears. I didn't feel any sort of pain; I wasn't even particularly lonely. Nothing existed but the free-falling world of sleep.

I'd feel a little lonely when I woke, but only for a moment. I'd look up at the overcast sky and realize just how much time had passed since I'd fallen asleep. *I wasn't even planning to sleep,* I'd think vaguely to myself, *and now I've gone and wasted the entire day.* Suddenly the heavy regret I felt, a regret that was almost shame, would be pierced by a cold blade of fear.

When exactly did I give myself over to sleep? When did I stop resisting . . . ? I used to be so lively, I was always wide awake—but when was that? So long ago it felt like ancient times. Like scenes out of the most distant past, panoramas of ferns and dinosaurs that spring roughly to the eye, vividly colored, my memories of that time always appeared to me as images shrouded in mist.

* * *

*B*ut even while I slept, even then I could tell when my boy-friend called.

The telephone sounded completely different when it was Mr. Iwanaga. For some reason I could just tell it was him. Every other sound came to me from far away, but when he called, the ringing of the phone reverberated deliciously inside my head, the way music does when you listen to it through head-phones. So I'd go and pick up the receiver, and that voice of his—a voice so deep it always startled me—would say my name.

"Terako?"

Yes, I'd reply in a tone so empty he'd chuckle.

And he'd say what he always said.

"Perhaps you were sleeping?"

He generally spoke more casually, so I loved to hear him say that, really loved it, those polite words coming out of the blue. Every time he said them I'd feel like the world had snapped shut. I went blind, as if some curtain had dropped. I savored the echoes of his voice for what seemed like an eternity.

Then at last I'd be completely awake.

"Yes, I was asleep."

Last time he called it was evening, and it was raining. The roar of the downpour and the leaden tone of that heavy sky had put a pall over the entire town. Just then, in the midst of all that, it occurred to me how extremely important his phone call was. I realized that nothing but that single line connected me to the outside world.

Then he'd start going on about when and where we should meet, and suddenly I'd be irritated. *Look, skip this stuff. Just say it again, that line I like so much: "Perhaps you were sleeping?" Encore!* I'd pretend to pound my feet on the floor as I scribbled out a note to myself. Yes, that's fine. Yes, I'll be there.

If someone could give me some sort of evidence that what we're doing here is really love, I'd be so tremendously relieved that I'd probably kneel down at that person's feet. And if it isn't love, if it's eventually going to end, I want to go on sleeping like this; I want to stop hearing the phone when he calls. Let me be alone again.

I spent the summer feeling like that, exhausted by my anxiety.

A year and a half had passed since we'd met.

"*A* friend of mine has died."

Two months had gone by and I still hadn't managed to say this. I knew he'd listen if I told him, really listen, so why did I keep holding back? Why? I didn't know.

Every night the thought plagued me.

Should I tell him? Should I start telling him right now?

I tried to find the words as we walked.

A friend of mine has died. I don't think you ever met her. Her name was Shiori, and she was the girl I got along with best.

She started doing this bizarre work after she graduated from college. I guess it was sort of like restrained prostitution, you know, a kind of service. But she was such a wonderful person. . . . We lived together when we were in college, in the same apartment I'm in now. And it was terrific. It was so much fun I could hardly believe it. We were never afraid of anything, we just spent every day talking about things, all kinds of things, and then sometimes we'd stay up all night, sometimes we'd get unbelievably drunk. Even if something really unpleasant happened while we were out, we'd come back home to the apartment and go crazy making jokes about it until finally we'd forgotten the whole thing. God, it was fun! We used to discuss my relationship with you a lot, you know. Except when I say "discuss" I mean things like, you know, maybe we'd talk about what a jerk you were, or else I'd go on and on about how happy you made me, it was just that kind of stuff, and she'd do the same. You know what I mean, right? Men and women can't be friends, right, that just can't happen. And by the time you start feeling totally comfortable together you're not really in love anymore, are you? But with Shiori that problem didn't exist, we just got along really well together. I don't know how to explain it, but when I was with her it was like, you know, like those times when life starts weighing down on you so much, it felt like that weight had been reduced by half. I just started feeling better, it wasn't like she did anything special or anything, I guess it was just that however relaxed we got, however much she and I let down our guards, things never got at all mushy, you know, she was gentle and kind just the right amount, that's what she was like. Women friends are the best, they really are. Back then I had you, and then I had Shiori, and to tell the truth that period was really hard for me. Though when I think back on all that now, it was really all just fun and games, it was like a big party. Every day I'd just laugh and cry and laugh and cry. Yeah, Shiori was a wonderful person, really great, she'd listen to you and she'd keep nodding and saying yeah, yeah, and there was always a bit of a smile hovering around her lips. And then she'd get these dimples. But she killed herself. She'd left my apartment a long time before that, she was living all by herself in this gorgeous place, and then she took a whole lot of sleeping pills and lay down in this tiny little single bed that she had there and just died. . . . She had a gigantic bed in the room she used for her work, this huge soft bed like you'd expect to find some medieval aristocrat falling asleep in, you know, a canopy over it and everything, and I really wonder why she didn't decide to die in that one. I guess there are some things even friends can't understand. You know I can even imagine her saying something about that, about how you'd probably have a better chance of going to heaven if you died in the big bed, it's just the sort of thing she might say. Her mother flew in from the country, and she called me up, and that's how I found out that Shiori had died. It was the first time I'd met her mother. She looked so much like Shiori I could hardly stand it. She asked me what sort of work Shiori had been doing, but in the end I couldn't even answer.

* * *

No, I just wouldn't be able to explain. The harder I would try to make him understand the more my words would turn to dust, the more they'd get caught up in their own momentum, a wind that would blow them out of existence—this much was clear to me, and so I said nothing. All those words I'd thought up wouldn't communicate a thing. Ultimately the only part that was true was the beginning. A friend of mine has died. How else was I supposed to express the loneliness I felt? How else could I make him see?

I stayed lost in thought as we walked along under the near-summer night sky. Then, as we crossed the large pedestrian bridge in front of the train station, he spoke.

"I can go to work in the afternoon tomorrow."

The lines of cars shimmered, one car after another, curving off into the distance. Suddenly it felt as if the night had become infinitely long, suddenly I felt happy. I found myself able to forget Shiori entirely.

"So we'll stay someplace tonight?"

I took his hand as I said this, unable to contain my joy.

His profile was graced, as always, by a small smile.

"Looks like it," he replied.

I was happy. I loved the night, I loved it so much it almost hurt. In the night everything seemed possible. I wasn't sleepy at all.

* * *

Sometimes when I was in bed with my boyfriend I would see the edge of night. The scenery there was unlike anything I'd ever encountered.

It didn't happen while we were doing it. Then it was just the two of us together, nothing separating us, no room for our minds to wander. He didn't speak during sex, he never said anything, and so I'd often fool around trying to get him to say this or that. But to tell the truth, I liked it that he kept quiet. It felt somehow like I was sleeping with an enormous night, just doing it through him. As long as he didn't use words it felt like I was embracing his true self, encircling it—a self that existed at a level much more profound than the actual man. Until we pulled our bodies apart, ready to fall asleep, I could get by without thinking of anything at all. I could just close my eyes and feel him, nothing but the true him.

I'd see it very late at night.

It made no difference whether it was a large hotel or a cheap motel like the ones you find behind train stations. Either way I'd wake up suddenly in the middle of the night, thinking I could hear the sounds of rain and wind.

I'd want so badly to see what it was like outside that I'd sit up and open the window. A bracingly cold wind would flow into the room, breaking through the hot air that filled it, and I'd see the stars blinking. Or perhaps a soft rain would be just starting to fall.

I'd go on looking out at all that for a while, and then I'd turn to look at him and see that he wasn't sleeping, that his eyes were wide open. For some reason I'd find myself unable to speak, and so I'd remain silent, simply gaze deep into his eyes. He shouldn't have been able to see outside, since he was lying down, but the look in his eyes was always so bright and clear it was like he'd taken it all in, all the sounds outside the window, all that scenery.

"How's the weather?" he'd ask me, very quietly.

And I'd answer that it was raining, or windy, or that it was so clear you could see the stars. Then I'd start feeling lonely, like I might be going sort of crazy. *Why do I feel so lonely when I'm with this guy?* I'd think. *Maybe it's because things between us are so complex? Or maybe it's because I have no feelings at all about our relationship except that I like it, because I have no clear sense of what I want us to be doing?*

The only thing I'd understood right from the very beginning was that our love was supported by loneliness. That neither one of us could haul ourselves up out of the deadly numbness we felt when we lay together, so silent, in darkness so isolating it seemed to shine.

This was the edge of night.

*T*he small company I'd been working for was so terribly busy that it was impossible for me to find time to see him, so I quit pretty soon. For almost half a year now I'd had nothing to do. My days were empty, and so for the most part I passed them relaxing, shopping for myself, doing laundry.

I did have some savings, though not much, and my boyfriend put an incredibly large sum of money into the bank for me each month—after all, he said, I'd quit my job for him—so living was easy. At first I was hesitant to accept this, thinking that it would seem too much like being his mistress, but then it's always been my policy to take what people offer me. In the end I decided to take the money and be glad. All of which is to say, maybe I slept so much simply because I had so much free time. I've no idea how many young women like this there are in the world, but I kind of wonder if those oddly vague people you see in department stores during the day, women who don't quite seem to be students or people who work on their own, might not be the same. I know very well that I used to be like that myself, that I used to walk around with the same utterly unfocused look in my eyes.

I was walking down the street like that one cloudless afternoon when I happened to run into a friend of mine.

"Hey, how've you been?" I said, running up to him.

He was one of my friends from college, a nice guy, extremely bright. Shiori had dated him for a while, though not for very long. They'd even lived together for a few months.

"Oh, pretty good," he said, smiling.

"What are you up to? Are you out on business?"

He was wearing a black shirt and cotton pants, the sort of clothes that looked like they were definitely meant for off the job. The only thing that suggested he was working was the single envelope he carried in his otherwise empty hand.

"Yeah, I'm just delivering this now. What about you? Looks like you're still as unoccupied as ever. . . ."

My friend often let the ends of his words trail off into nothing, in a way that sounded really gentle. He was grinning, there under the blue sky.

"That's right. I'm not doing a thing," I said.

"Living the life of luxury."

"Exactly. Hey, you're going to the subway, right? I'll come with you as far as the corner."

We started walking.

The blue sky was carved up to fit the shapes of the buildings lining the street, and it shone with a peculiar clarity. For some time now I'd been feeling like I was in some other country. Every once in a while the city streets at noon and the sunlight that washes over them make my memories and all sorts of things get muddled, especially in the very middle of summer. I could almost feel the skin on my arms burning, little by little.

"God it's hot."

"It is hot, isn't it?"

"I hear . . . I hear Shiori died," said my friend. "I heard just recently."

"That's right. Her parents came up from the country and everything. It was all really crazy," I said, realizing as I said it that it was a strange response.

"I can imagine. She had some kind of job, right? Something bizarre?"

"Yeah, it was a little bizarre. I hadn't even known such a job existed."

"Was that why she died? Because of her job?"

"Well . . . I don't know. But I don't think so."

"Yeah, I guess that's something only she would know. I mean, she was always smiling, you know? And she was such a wonderful person. I just can't see how she could have been in such pain that she felt she had to die."

"Me neither."

We settled into silence for a time as we descended the wide street that led down the hill, walking slowly side by side. Several cars drove past us, and dazzling streams of sunlight hit us straight on. *This man walking beside me has access to the same images of Shiori that I do, scenes only those of us who lived with her can know . . . Shiori with damp hair, Shiori cutting her nails, Shiori seen from behind as she washes the dishes, Shiori's sleeping face bathed in the morning sun.* Somehow this seemed very strange to me.

"So are you still as amoral as ever?" he said suddenly, grinning.

"Well that's a nice thing to say!" I replied, grinning back at him. "But I still am. We haven't broken up yet and he's still married."

"You really ought to try having a serious relationship, you know." My friend's voice was bright, without any sort of undertone at all, but this only made its impact stronger. "But then you were always mature for your age, weren't you? I guess you just like people older than you."

"Right. That's it." I smiled.

Though I was actually so serious about the relationship it frightened me, so serious my hands and legs started trembling whenever I considered what things would be like if it ended. And my emotions still continued to smolder, even though my boyfriend and I could have broken up at any time without it seeming at all strange.

"Well, see you later. Call me if there's a party or anything."

We'd reached the entrance to the subway. My friend raised his hand as he spoke, then descended the dimly lit stairs underground. I stood there in the burning sunlight watching his back until it vanished, feeling a little sad, unwilling to part. It felt like all the brightness inside me had slipped down the stairs with that back. I was alone in a sprawling emptiness.

Shiori came tumbling into my apartment almost immediately after she broke up with this friend of ours. She had an allowance, and she was the kind of person who preferred to live a very well-ordered life, but for some reason she didn't like the idea of living in any one place. And every time she moved she'd throw away everything she had, even her books, even presents she had received. She said it irritated her to have too much baggage. All she brought with her from our friend's apartment was her pillow, a terry-cloth blanket, and a single overnight bag. She wasn't one of those people who can't handle being alone, not at all, but she was constantly drifting from one friend's house to the next. It seemed to be something of a hobby.

"So why did you break up?" I asked her.

"Well, you know. I mean, I was the one sponging off him, right? So if I didn't go, there wouldn't be much he could do, would there?"

It was a vague reply.

"What did you like about him?" I asked.

"The way he speaks makes him sound so gentle, you know?" she said, and smiled a little nostalgically. "But once I was actually living with him, let me tell you, I found out he doesn't always talk like that. It's a lot more fun living with you. After all, you're always gentle, right?"

Shiori grinned again. White cheeks, hazy eyes—when she smiled, her face looked almost exactly like a marshmallow. We were still in college then, commuting between the apartment and school, yet no matter how much time we spent together—and our daily schedules were almost the same—we never fought. Before either one of us knew it, Shiori had come to feel completely at home in my apartment. Her presence had come to seem so natural it was as if she were diffused into the air.

There were times when I was with Shiori when it would occur to me that I really liked women a whole lot more than I liked men. I don't mean this in a lesbian sense, but it's something I felt very strongly. That's how good a person she was, and how much fun it was living with her. She was fair and slightly plump, her eyes were very narrow, her chest was large. You certainly couldn't have called her a beauty, and her manner was so mild that you couldn't help thinking of someone's mother when you saw her—she was the type of person who completely lacked what's generally known as sex appeal. She spoke very little; she was precisely what a woman is supposed to be. When I thought of her it was always the soft shadow of her presence that came to me, not her appearance: the sense of how I felt when she was there. Sometimes, back when she was still living with me, I'd look at her smile—which somehow seemed to cast only the very palest of shadows, to be always on the verge of vanishing forever—or at the deep wrinkles that gathered around the corners of her eyes, and I'd feel an inexplicable yearning to bury my head in her giant breasts and sob and sob and tell her absolutely everything. The bad things, the lies I'd told, things about the future, how tired I felt, all the things I'd put up with, the darkness of night, my uneasiness—everything. And then I'd want to turn my thoughts back, to linger over memories of my mother and father, of the moon above the town where I grew up, of the color of the winds that moved over the fields.

That's the sort of person Shiori was.

*T*hough it was a very brief encounter, that meeting with my old friend left my head in a state of chaos. Somehow I made my way alone through sunlight that made me feel faint, and arrived at my apartment. My apartment gets a lot of sun in the afternoon. I stood in the dazzling light, my mind blank, taking the laundry off the line. A pleasant, just-washed scent drifted up from the white sheets as they brushed my cheek.

I started feeling sleepy. Light came streaming down over my back like water in a shower while I folded the clothes, and at the same time the cold air from the air conditioner blew over me. I started to doze off. Naps that begin this way feel terrific. You feel as if you're about to have a dream all in gold. I slipped out of my skirt and slid into bed. Lately I hadn't been dreaming at all. Soon everything would go black.

Suddenly the ringing of the phone came spiraling into my sleep, and I was jolted back into consciousness. *That's him calling,* I thought, then sat up in bed and glanced over at the clock. Not even ten minutes had passed since I'd fallen asleep. Somehow I never even noticed when calls came from other people, I just went on sleeping. If things as minor as this came under the heading of ESP, I guess I'd have fairly impressive supernatural powers.

"Terako?" he said when I lifted the receiver.

"Yes, it's me."

"Perhaps you were sleeping?" he asked, sounding vaguely pleased. I smiled to myself unthinkingly.

"I was just about to get up."

"I'll bet. So, you want to go for dinner tonight?"

"Yeah, sounds good."

"Okay. How about seven-thirty, the usual place?"

"All right."

The room was still filled with light, still steeped in silence when I hung up the phone. All the shadows cast on the floor were dark and clearly outlined; I was in a time cut off from the rest of the world. I kept staring at the shadows for a while, but I didn't feel like doing anything, so in the end I got back into bed. This time I thought about Shiori a little before I slept.

The guy I'd met earlier, Shiori's last boyfriend, had asked me whether she'd died "because of her job." And though I'd told him I didn't know, it had occurred to me then that in a certain distant sense it was probably true.

Shiori had been completely absorbed in her work, it had possessed her. That's why she'd moved out of my apartment. And I really do believe that in some sense she had found her calling in that job, that it was work only she could do. She'd gotten a part-time job in a bar on an introduction from some friend. Apparently she was noticed by a customer who worked as a scout for an organization that ran this sort of secret club—or perhaps it would be more accurate to say that it specialized in a peculiar form of prostitution. All she had to do was lie beside her customers in bed. I was surprised myself the first time I heard it.

The apartment she used for her work was just downstairs from the one her patron-employer rented for her, and the "work" apartment was where the huge, very sleepable double bed was located. I actually saw the place once. Being there was more like being in a foreign country than in a hotel or something. It had a real bedroom, a place meant for sleeping, the kind of room I'd only seen in movies. Several times a week Shiori lay there alongside her customers until morning.

"*What*? You mean you don't have sex?" I asked.

This was the night Shiori confessed that she'd gotten so deeply involved in her work that she wanted to move out, that she'd be getting an apartment with a place where she could work.

"Of course not! People who want that stuff go other places." Shiori smiled gently.

"I had no idea such a job even existed. But then I guess that's supply and demand, isn't it?" There was no way for me to stop her if she'd decided to leave. And I could tell that in some way I didn't really understand, she had become a prisoner of her work, of that peculiar job.

"I'll miss you," I said.

"You'll come visit me, right?" she replied. "After all, my apartment is just an ordinary apartment."

She hadn't even started to pack, so it was still difficult for me to grasp the fact that she was leaving, that this woman, who seemed so much a part of my home, was leaving. We sat together on the floor like we always did until very late that night, half watching music videos, commenting on them from time to time, saying that a certain song was good, that a certain singer was ugly. Time always seemed to become strangely distorted when I was with Shiori. This was because of her eyes. She had an extremely gentle face, but her narrow eyes were always as cloudy and dark as a blue moon.

Sometimes she'd spread her futon out on the floor next to my bed and go to sleep, and I'd turn out the lights and be able to see her perfectly white arm lying there in the moonlight, its outline absolutely clear. But often we'd talk even more after I turned out the lights. It amazes me to think how much we talked. The night she told me she was leaving, Shiori told me a whole lot about her job. I listened to her tiny voice as it flowed on through the dark like a melody played on some musical instrument.

"All night long I'm not allowed to sleep. I mean just imagine, what if the person next to me woke up in the middle of the night and I was sleeping, you know, just snoring away? My work wouldn't be worth very much then, it wouldn't be professional, see what I mean? Whatever happens I can't let the person feel lonely. Everyone who comes—and I only take people with references from others—is very respectable, very rich. They've all been hurt in unbelievably subtle ways, they're all exhausted. So exhausted they don't even realize they're exhausted. These people always wake up in the middle of the night, absolutely always. I'm not exaggerating when I say that. And it's really important that I smile at them then, in that pallid light. I hand them a glass of ice water. Sometimes they want some coffee or something, so I go right into the kitchen and make it for them. Most of the time, when you do that, they calm down and just fall asleep again I think all these people, all they want is to have someone there, lying next to them. Some of them are women, some of them are foreigners. But I'm not very reliable, you know, sometimes I fall asleep. . . . Because when you're sleeping next to all these exhausted people, it's like you start matching your breath to theirs, slowly, those deep breaths . . . maybe you're breathing in the darkness they have inside them. Sometimes I'm thinking to myself *You mustn't go to sleep* even as I'm dozing off, having some terrible dream. All these surreal things. Dreams where I'm on a boat that's going under, dreams where I've lost some coins I was collecting, dreams where the dark comes in through the window and blocks up my throat—my heart is pounding, I'm so scared, and then I wake up. It's really frightening. The person beside me is still asleep, and I look at them and think, *Yes, of course, what I've just seen is how this person feels inside, so lonely it hurts, such desolation.* Yeah, it really scares me."

Shiori was staring straight up through the moonlight. The whites of her eyes seemed to shine faintly, and it occurred to me that this was how she was feeling inside, but for some reason I couldn't bring myself to say it. But I was sure it was true. I wanted to cry, I was so sure it was true.

Already the summer was half over. Somehow it seemed wrong for my boyfriend to be wearing short sleeves, and I was shocked to see his bare arms when he arrived at the shop where we met. I guess I just always imagined him dressed in a sweater and coat, maybe because we'd met in winter. I'd always feel like we were out walking in a north wind when we got together. I thought I'd gone crazy. We'd be inside some shop with the air conditioner on full blast, it would be a stiflingly hot tropical night outdoors, yet deep down I'd still feel just the same.

"Shall we go?" he said, staring at me, evidently puzzled by the fact that I'd simply followed him with my eyes until he was right in front of me. But I still sat there gazing up into his eyes, my mind completely blank.

"Right, okay," I said, and stood up.

For some reason my mind always went blank the instant we met.

"So what did you do today?" he asked vaguely, as he always did.

"I was at home. . . . Oh, I ran into an old friend today."

"A guy? Maybe you had a date?" he said, grinning.

So I replied, grinning back, "Yeah, it was a young guy."

"Was it really?" He sulked a little. There was only six years' difference between us, but that gap bothered him strangely. I have a feeling that this was because my appearance was unusually childish, so much so that when I went out without makeup I'd sometimes be mistaken for a high school student. It was as if I hadn't aged at all since I left college. No doubt this had something to do with the way I lived.

"You're free tonight?" I asked.

He looked sadly into my eyes. "Actually I've got to go see some relatives," he said, sounding very apologetic. "We'll just have dinner, okay?"

"Relatives? Some of yours?"

"No. My in-laws."

He no longer even tried to hide it from me. Maybe he'd realized that my instincts were just too good, that I could tell? My boyfriend had a wife.

An unconscious wife, a wife who lay quietly asleep in the hospital.

*W*inter was at its very coldest the first time he and I arranged to meet. We drove to the beach. It was the Sunday after I'd quit my job, and Mr. Iwanaga—he'd been one of my bosses at work—had asked me out on a date. I was more or less aware that he was married. It was a long, long day.

Thinking back over everything now, I can see that some kind of major change was taking place inside me even then. Somewhere within the borders of that day I left behind the healthy young woman I'd been, and came on without her. Nothing had changed, not really, and yet before the day was over we found ourselves being dragged into the flow of some gigantic, dark, irresistible fate: the two of us together. And I'm not just talking about the sexual energy people feel when they fall in love. It was something much bigger than that, and it was something incredibly sad. A current so strong even our combined strength was powerless against it.

But to tell the truth I was still feeling cheery then, I was bursting with energy, and we hadn't even kissed, and I adored him more than anyone else in the world. He was at the wheel, and we kept driving on and on along the road that traced the shore, and the ocean was beautiful, and as the waves rolled in the sunlight I felt this overwhelming energy surge up shimmering within me. I was as happy as I could be.

We went down to the beach and walked a bit. The insides of my shoes quickly became filled with sand. But even so the breeze blowing in off the ocean felt good, the sunlight was soft. It was so cold that we couldn't stay out very long, and knowing this made the sound of the waves even more precious. Suddenly I remembered something. I bent my head back and gazed up into his face.

"So what's your wife like, Mr. Iwanaga?" I asked teasingly.

My boyfriend smiled wryly. "She's a vegetable."

This makes me sound completely unrepentant, I know, but whenever I think of that question of mine and his response I just burst out laughing.

So what's your wife like? She's a vegetable.

Of course at the time I couldn't laugh. I just opened my eyes very wide and said, "Huh?"

"She got in a car accident and she's been in the hospital ever since. I guess it's been about a year. That's why I can go around on dates like this, you know, take a gal out on a Sunday."

He spoke brightly, pleasantly. He had one of his hands stuffed deep down in his pocket. I took hold of it and pulled it out. It felt very hot.

"That can't be true," I said, startled.

"There's not much point in telling a lie like that, is there?"

"No, I guess not." I wrapped both his hands in mine. "Do you go visit her and take care of her and stuff? Is it very hard?"

"Let's talk about something else," he said, averting his eyes. "When a married man's having an affair you can be pretty sure he's showing up at dates with about a ton of stuff weighing down on him. That much is true even if his wife isn't a vegetable."

"Another tasteless joke," I said.

I raised one of his hands to my cheek, and the sound of the wind disappeared. The scent of winter rose to my nostrils. Off in the distance clouds glimmered over the ocean. They were melting into the sky, turning purple. The crash of the waves echoed faintly through his palm.

"Let's go," I said. "It's cold out here. Let's go get some tea."

I started to draw my hand away, perfectly naturally, but he squeezed it tightly in his, ever so tightly, just for a moment. I was surprised, and glanced up, and then I saw the color in his eyes—eyes that were deeper than the ocean, that could have been staring right into infinity—and it felt as if all kinds of things had become clear to me.

For an instant I saw what was there between us in all its complexity, for an instant I understood: I knew everything about him, I saw the fantastic love that was growing up between us. And that's when I really started to love him. All at once the halfhearted attraction I'd felt for him changed—at that instant, as we stood with the ocean before us—into full-fledged, total love.

I was the one who kept worrying about the time while we ate.

"Shouldn't you be going?" I asked, then asked again about three more times. It occurred to me that not many relatives would come to pay a visit after eight o'clock at night.

"Listen, if I say I have time, I have time," he said, spinning the round Chinese-style lazy Susan farther than he needed to, smiling. "Eat! Eat! You might as well just stop worrying."

"I can't eat if you're spinning it."

The sight of all that food whirling by under my eyes, circling with such energy that it almost could have been a merry-go-round, made me giggle. A waiter standing some distance away glowered at us.

"But really, it's okay. I'm driving there myself, and I'll be spending the night . . . besides, I've already told them that I'll be late because I have work. And they're also wonderful people. Really wonderful."

"That's what's so terrific about marriage," I said. "All these wonderful people used to be strangers, and now they're your relatives. It's great."

"You're not being ironic, are you?" he said, looking uneasy.

"Not at all," I replied.

And I wasn't. It's just that it was all so distant from me that I couldn't feel connected to it.

"Is . . . I mean . . . was your wife a wonderful person, too?"

Evidently there was no longer any possibility that she would wake up. According to my boyfriend, it was just a matter of talking things through now, of coming to grips with the situation.

"Yes, she was a wonderful person. She was very well brought up, she had a nice crisp air about her, you know, and the smallest things moved her to tears. And she was always in a hurry, and she was a terrible driver, and that's why she got into an accident. Is that enough? Do you think we could stop talking about her now?"

"Okay."

This whole business with his wife didn't disturb me that much, and I'd told him that, but my boyfriend still hated talking about her—hated it with startling vehemence and consistency. I was drinking a sweet liqueur that tasted of apricot. I was starting to get drunk, but for some reason I wasn't at all sleepy. I was coming to see my boyfriend with increasing clarity as he sat there across the table from me. And I understood. None of us are born between the branches of trees. My boyfriend had parents, and his wife had parents, and I was sure that hers must be immersed in their grief. I thought of all the many hard facts that one has to deal with when one is drawn into sudden misfortune—the hospitals and the attendants, the expenses, the divorce, the family register, the decision to let the person die. . . . All this really exists.

Sometimes I felt like bursting out and telling him that I understood all that. I wanted so badly to say it. Because I knew that he'd be shocked if I did, and that it would make him reconsider certain things. . . .

So you want to be totally involved in all that stuff, right? You want to be there for your wife right up until the very end, and you want everyone to feel like they can rely on you. But you know you're not helping anyone. It's just that you'd never be able to forgive yourself if you left. You're a pretty cool guy, right, and you're going to keep doing whatever it takes so that you can go on thinking you're cool, and at the same time work things out so that your love for your wife fits in with all that. And then there's me. You know very well that I'm here watching you, and that even though none of this is any of my business I can still see how really cool you're being, and to tell the truth I can't accept that this is none of my business because I'm too nice, because it does hurt me—but of course you know that, too. The truth is that you're an extremely cold person. But even so—you can tell, right? That I just love this, the way you're dealing with things. . . . That I'm so crazy about it I can hardly stand it. Come to think of it, I guess maybe I've gotten swept up in all of this somehow, at some point, without noticing. Yeah, I guess I have.

But every time my thoughts reached this point, every time, my desire to speak would vanish. And so we remained precisely as we were, making no waves, at a standstill. He and the others passed their nights and days talking through issues of life and death, lending support to one another, and I passed my days in silence, as if I were his mistress, and his wife went on sleeping.

And all along, right from the first, a certain phrase had been spinning back and forth through my head. *This love of ours isn't real.* The feeling that these words evoked in me was like a premonition of something awful. The more exhausted my boyfriend became, the more he tried to keep me at a distance from reality. He never actually came out and said anything about this, so I'm sure that it was just an unconscious desire, but he tried his best to keep me from working, and he preferred it when I stayed in my apartment and lived life in silence, and when we met in town our meetings were like the shadow of a dream. He dressed me in beautiful clothes, and he liked it when I laughed and cried just a little, very softly. But then . . . no, I can't say that it was just him. I'd absorbed the darkness of his exhaustion—I liked acting that way. There was something lonely between us, and we protected that ever so carefully in the way we loved each other. And so things were fine as they were. For the time being this was fine.

* * *

"Shall I drive you home?" he said.

We'd left the restaurant and were heading for the parking lot.

"I love it when you say stuff like that. Sort of extra polite," I replied.

"No doubt you do, Mademoiselle." He laughed.

"I don't think you got quite the right nuance that time." I laughed too. "Anyway, it's still early, I can just walk home. It'll help me sober up."

"Yeah, I guess."

His voice sounded a little glum. In the darkness his face looked terribly thin. The long lines of cars were bathed in a silence so profound it was awful. It felt as if the parking lot were at the very edge of the world. Things always felt a little like this when we parted.

"God, you really look old right now," I teased.

He answered as he climbed into his car, looking very earnest. "I'm so worn out I really don't know what's what anymore, you know? But I guess it's just a matter of time now. That's a really rude thing to say, and it'd be just as rude no matter who I was saying it to. But at the moment I can't even think about what's coming, I just can't."

He said this almost as if he were talking to himself.

"Right, I understand. It's okay." I said this very quickly and then shut the car door. I didn't want to hear any more. I started walking down the dark night road, and he steered his car up alongside me and then drove on, tapping the horn. I laughed and waved, but suddenly I started feeling like the Cheshire cat, as if there were nothing left of me now but my grinning face, hanging there in the darkness.

I've always liked getting drunk and walking the streets at night, whether there's a lover walking at my side or not. Moonlight fills the entire town, the shadows of buildings stretch on forever. The rhythm of my footsteps and the distant rumble of the cars merge. At midnight the sky over the city is strangely bright, and you feel a little uneasy, but at the same time perfectly safe.

Though my feet were taking me back toward home, I was dimly aware that my true self wasn't at all inclined to go back. No, I knew what I wanted. I was heading for Shiori's apartment. On nights like this I always stopped by her apartment. Not the one she used for her work, but the one she lived in. I don't know if it's because I was drunk or because I'd been sleeping too much, but I could sense that the line separating recollection from reality was starting to become dangerously thin. There was something a little odd about me lately. Even now I couldn't help feeling that if I just stepped into the elevator in her building and went up to her apartment I'd be certain to find her at home.

Yes, often after my boyfriend and I had been out on one of these vaguely lonely, listless dates, I'd go see Shiori.

* * *

Come to think of it, being with him always made me feel incredibly lonely. I don't know why, but for some reason I'd always end up having these vaguely melancholy thoughts circling through my head—the kind of thoughts that you have when you're gazing up at the moon, full of longing, watching as it sinks deeper and deeper into the blue depths of night, as it shimmers way off in the distance. The sort of thoughts that make you feel like you've been dyed completely blue, all the way to the tips of your toenails.

Being with him turned me into a woman who didn't speak.

I tried to explain this to Shiori, but no matter how valiantly I tried I just couldn't convince her that someone as talkative as I am could ever be quiet. But it was true. Whenever we got together I would listen to him talk, and then I'd nod, and that was it. The rhythm of my nods and the rhythm of his talking would become so exquisitely well synchronized that it almost became a sort of art. And that's when I started getting the feeling that what I was doing was a lot like Shiori's job, like lying next to people as they slept.

I tried to tell her about this once. "I don't know why, but for some reason it always feels like the middle of winter when we're in bed together."

"Oh, I know. I know!" Shiori said.

"What do you mean you know? How can you know when you haven't even heard what I'm saying?" I said, getting angry.

"Hey, I'm a pro," Shiori said, narrowing her eyes. "You see, people like him think everything that's not formally declared is basically nil."

"Nil?"

"That's why he's so nervous. As soon as he starts thinking of the two of you as a unit, his situation becomes extremely dangerous, you see? So for the time being you're nil, you're being held in reserve, the pause button is pressed down, you're stacked in the stockroom, you're life's special bonus."

"I . . . I think I know what you mean, but . . . what's this 'nil'? What kind of a place does he put me in, you know? Inside him?"

"Somewhere completely dark," Shiori said.

And then she laughed.

I really did want to see Shiori. And so, though there was obviously no way we could meet, I kept plodding aimlessly along, taking a long way home. Somehow this made me feel like I was getting closer to her. The numbers of people on the street gradually decreased. The night seemed to thicken.

The last time I went to Shiori's apartment was about two weeks before she died, and that ended up being the last time I ever saw her. It was another one of these occasions where I'd started feeling a little down and had just dropped by, without any warning, in the middle of the night. Shiori was there, and she welcomed me very cheerfully, very brightly.

But what I saw when I walked in caught me by surprise. There was an enormous hammock hanging in the very center of the living room.

"What's that for?" I asked, pointing up at it from where I was standing in the entryway. "Do you keep stuff in there or something?"

"No, it's just that I lie in that really fluffy bed when I'm working, you know? Except that I've got to stay awake, right?" Her voice was the same as always—high and soft and fragile. "So now the second I get into any sort of bed my eyes pop wide open. I thought I might be able to sleep in this thing, you know, since there's no way to get comfortable in it. . . ."

It made sense once she'd explained it. And so, thinking that every job has its own problems, I walked in and sat down on the sofa.

"Do you want some tea? Or maybe something alcoholic?"

Shiori's leisurely gestures and the little smile that always flitted at the corners of her mouth were wonderfully familiar. I felt the incomprehensible exhaustion that had been building up inside me slipping away, just as it had when she'd lived in my apartment.

"Something alcoholic," I said.

"Well then, maybe I'll open a bottle of gin."

Shiori took lots of ice from the freezer and put it in a dish, cut a lemon, and brought out an unopened bottle of gin.

"You don't mind opening it?" I asked.

I was almost buried in the sofa. I picked up my glass.

"Not a bit. I hardly ever drink."

She was sipping orange juice. The room was strangely quiet.

"It's quiet here, isn't it?" I said.

I wasn't getting at all drunk, I just felt completely calm. I wasn't feeling sad about anything in particular, so there was nothing for me to say.

"Has something happened?" Shiori kept asking. She sounded extremely eager, like someone's loyal dog.

And I replied, "No, not really." But the moment I said this I realized how grave it sounded. "Nothing's wrong, really. I guess I was just thinking, you know . . . don't you watch TV anymore, or listen to music?"

Shiori's apartment truly was quiet that night. Every sound but our two voices slid off into nothing, as if we were huddled inside an igloo on some snowbound night. The thinness of Shiori's voice only emphasized the silence.

"Not really," Shiori said. "Why, is it too quiet for you?"

"Don't be silly. I'm not the sort of person who comes to visit and then complains like that. I'm not that rude," I said. "I just have this feeling like something's wrong with my ears."

"Recently every little noise has been bothering me," Shiori said. Her eyes were utterly empty. "But seriously, what's wrong? Does it have something to do with Mr. Iwanaga? Did you have an argument about his wife? I can always tell when you're feeling depressed, you know. We did live together."

"No, everything's still the same. Nothing has—it's just that I'm . . ." I shuddered at what I'd been about to say. It was something horrible.

It's just that I'm tired of waiting.

"It's just . . . ?"

"That I'm afraid I've been telling him some lies. And we had a bit of an argument because of that, you know, that's all. Nothing's changed. He doesn't like talking about his wife, but it sounds as if having to deal with her relatives is pretty hard for him, and that's only natural, and it seems like he goes to the hospital a lot. But I really don't mind. Not at all."

"Really? Well then, that's all right," Shiori said, smiling. "You know, I really hope the two of you stay together like this, on good terms. I was in on this relationship right from the start, after all."

"Don't worry. We won't break up."

It's strange, but I started feeling increasingly sure of myself as I said this, so that before long I felt completely carefree. I don't really remember what we talked about after that. That's how casual it all was. Just memories of our life together, stories from work, tidbits about makeup and about programs on TV, that sort of stuff . . . and all the time that hammock was hovering there in the space behind my head. Shiori's white shirt, water coming to a boil in her red kettle, steam rising over the hot green tea we drank, yes, that's all I remember now, just things like that.

"Well, I'm off." I stood up.

"Why don't you sleep over?" Shiori asked.

It was tempting, but somehow the idea that I'd get to sleep in the bed while Shiori took the hammock made me feel a bit uncomfortable—after all, I was the guest. I decided to go home.

"Do you feel any better?" Shiori asked in the entryway.

For the first time that evening I swallowed my pride.

"Yes, I really do."

Shiori's eyes narrowed.

"Maybe you need me to come sleep with you?" she said.

Evidently she was teasing me.

"Sure, if you like," I said.

I laughed and walked out of her apartment.

The door closed. I took two or three steps towards the elevator . . . and then suddenly I felt something tugging me violently back, as if someone had pulled me by the hair. I yearned to see her face once more, but even if I turned around again—she was already on the far side of that iron door, she'd already stepped back into her own time, I could feel it, and besides there was nothing I wanted to say, nothing to say even if I did go back. And so I just walked into the elevator. . . .

I was still a long way from my apartment when I became too exhausted to go on walking, and so like an idiot I ended up taking a taxi back. And then I dropped off into a deep sleep, I was sucked into a darkness that was perfectly black, in which I had no thoughts at all. A sleep so profound it was as if some switch had been flicked off.

Nothing exists in this world but me and my bed. . . .

* * *

*S*uddenly the telephone rang, jolting me from sleep. Already sunlight was streaming through the window, and the room was bright.

It's him. I lifted the receiver.

"Have you been out?" he asked immediately.

His voice sounded strange, different from usual.

"No."

I glanced at the clock. It was two in the afternoon. I couldn't believe how soundly I'd slept. I'd gone to sleep long before midnight the night before.

The voice that came through the receiver sounded unconvinced.

"You've really been there all along?"

"I really have. I was asleep."

"I called a few times, but you didn't pick up. It seemed kind of odd."

He sounded as if he still wasn't quite sure what to think. I was pretty surprised myself. *Here I'd been thinking I had these supernatural powers . . . maybe they've started breaking down?* It had never even occurred to me that things might progress to the point where I'd no longer be able to tell when my boyfriend called; that hadn't even seemed like a possibility. I started feeling extremely uneasy. But I spoke cheerfully even so.

"God, I didn't even notice. I just went right on sleeping."

"Oh. Anyway, you and I didn't get to talk very much yesterday, so I thought maybe we could get together again tomorrow. . . . "

My boyfriend was generally pretty blunt, but he'd never come right out and suggest that we go spend the night somewhere or say that he wanted to have sex with me or anything like that. That was another thing that I kind of liked about him.

"Okay, that'll be fine."

I never tell my boyfriend that I'm busy when I'm not. No matter how effective they are, cheap techniques like that just don't agree with me. So it's always okay, it's always all right. In my opinion the surest way to hook a man is to be as open with him as possible.

"I'll get a room, then," he said, and hung up.

Once again I was alone in my apartment. It was late in the afternoon. Too much sleep had left me feeling a little dizzy.

Ever since I was a child I've been good at falling asleep. I suppose one of my most impressive points—apart from the knack I have for identifying phone calls from my boyfriend—is that I can fall asleep whenever I want. As a kind of hobby, my mother worked nights at a snack bar run by one of her friends, and though my father was just an ordinary businessman he had a peculiarly large streak of generosity, so that he not only thought it was okay for my mother to do work like that, but even stopped by the bar fairly often. Since I was an only child, I ended up spending most nights at home alone. And since our house was much too big for a child to stay in all by herself, I made it my policy just to hold my breath and count to three and hurl myself headlong into sleep. The thoughts that twirled through my head when I turned out the bedroom lights and lay there gazing up at the dark ceiling were always so deliciously sweet and full of loneliness that I hated them. I didn't want to start liking that loneliness, so before I knew it I'd be asleep.

The first time I started remembering all this as an adult was after my boyfriend and I spent our first night together, as we were driving back. We'd gone up and spent the night in Kanagawa Prefecture, done a bit of sight-seeing the next day, and then started back in the evening. I'm not sure why, but somehow the fact that the day was about to end really terrified me, left me wallowing in despair. I sat in the car, cursing all the green lights, and every time we got caught at a red light I'd feel a gush of relief, and a wave of joy would surge up within me. It was extremely hard to have to return to Tokyo and then head back again to our separate lives, our individual daily routines. I suppose this was because we'd just slept together for the first time, and—yes, this most of all—because I'd been thinking about his wife the whole time. I'd never felt this nervous before. I kept imagining the moment when I'd arrive back at my apartment, when I'd be all alone again, and every time I'd get so scared it felt like my skin was being peeled away.

I was sinking down into the depths of the scene before me, into those long lines of continuing lights—that's how I felt. My body shrank into itself. I can't really explain why I felt so lonely. My boyfriend was the same as always, just as gentle and kind as always, and he was cracking jokes, and I was laughing. But the fear never went away. It felt as if I were turning into ice.

At some point as we were going along like that, for whatever reason, I fell asleep. You could almost hear a little splash as I dropped off, that's how sudden it was. I had no idea when it happened. All I remember is his shaking me awake a few moments later, saying that we'd arrived. I realized then that we were parked in front of my building.

Oh, that was great. That wasn't bad at all!

The few minutes I'd expected to be the saddest and most painful of all had vanished in a puff of smoke, and so having reached the point where it was necessary to say good-bye— and now that the time had come I could see that it was really nothing at all—I just smiled and waved back at him. *Yes, sleep is on my side,* I thought. Once more I was amazed.

Yet lately a certain question had been fluttering through my head right at the moment I awoke. *But isn't this eating away at my life?* I began to feel a little bit afraid. It wasn't just that I'd started sleeping right through my boyfriend's calls, utterly oblivious to the ringing, it was also that recently I'd been settling into a sleep so profound that, every time I woke, it was like I'd died and was just returning to life—I could almost believe that, and sometimes it even occurred to me that if I were able to look at myself while I slept, all I'd see would be my perfectly white bones, nothing else. Sometimes I'd find myself in a dazzled haze, wondering if maybe it wouldn't be best for me just to rot away as I lay there, without ever waking; to slip away to that place called eternity. It occurred to me that I might be possessed by sleep, just as Shiori had been possessed by her work. The thought scared me.

*M*y boyfriend never spoke in any detail about what was happening, but lately when we were in bed together I could sense how utterly exhausted everything was making him. He didn't tell me anything specific about how things were with his wife, and on top of that I don't know the first thing about medicine, so I can't be sure that this is right, but I'm guessing that his wife's family probably wanted to keep her alive no matter what, and since my boyfriend said they were all "wonderful people," I'm sure they must have told him that he should feel free to apply for a divorce if he wanted one. But every time he went to the hospital his wife was still lying there sleeping, and so he'd think, *She's still alive,* and that must have been really painful for him, terribly painful, and I'm guessing that he'd feel he had a kind of duty not to leave her *until she dies,* that it was this kind of attitude that made him sort of cool, that made people respect him. And of course he couldn't tell anyone about me. He'd been so worn out by everything that was going on that he couldn't have married me soon even if it had all ended, and he was wondering how much longer I'd be willing to go on seeing him with things as they were, and that made him uneasy, just as Shiori had said. *Yes, yes, in the* *end it's always the same. It turns into a vicious circle. The only thing I can do for him now is not say anything. All I can do is worry that he'll come down on me too heavily, now that he's on top. He's just gotten older and older during the year and a half we've been together, but nothing I can do will stop that.* Maybe it's because I was exhausted myself, I don't know, but I'd be in a sort of haze the whole time we were doing it, just thinking thoughts like these, and it didn't feel good at all. It felt like the darkness that filled the room was seeping down into me. The electrified town glittered brightly through the thin curtain, stretching on and on through the darkness, looking as far off as a dream. I found myself gazing outside every time I turned. I thought of the vast growl of cold wind that was probably blowing across the roofs.

*W*e were lying side by side, falling asleep. Suddenly he spoke.

"How many years have you lived alone?"

"What? Me?"

His question was so completely unexpected that I shouted. The lights of cars passing by outside glimmered softly on the floor, which somehow took his question and whirled it around, leaving me momentarily bewildered, my memories of past and of recent events hopelessly mixed up.

Huh? What? Why am I here? What have I been doing all this time? For a moment I couldn't remember anything about the time before my boyfriend and I got together.

"Oh, oh, right. . . . Just a year, actually. Before that I was living with this friend of mine, you know? Another woman."

"Really? Actually, now that you mention it, I remember there used to be some girl who'd answer the phone every once in a while when I called. What's she doing now?"

I told him a peculiar lie. "She married. She ran off and left me."

"That wasn't very nice," he said, laughing.

He lay there on his back. I watched his broad chest move. Suddenly, quite casually, I asked him a question.

"Do you think your wife would be mad if she knew?"

His face stiffened a little, then gradually softened into a smile.

"Not at all. Of course if she were conscious it's pretty unlikely that this would have gotten as far as it has, you know, so you can't really tell, but if she could see the position I'm in right now, and if she could see what you're like, I doubt she'd be mad. That's the kind of person she was."

"A wonderful woman?"

"Yeah. I really think I've been blessed where women are concerned. I mean you're wonderful, and she was a wonderful woman too. . . . But then she's no longer in this world, is she? Not anymore."

Hearing him make this statement in his sleepy voice scared me, and I fell silent. For some reason those words made me shiver. Then as I lay there watching, my boyfriend drifted off to sleep, all alone, his breathing calm, and I stared at his closed eyelids, and listened to those deep breaths, and it began to seem like I might see all the way into his dreams.

A single consciousness wandering all alone in a distant night.

"You start matching your breath to theirs, slowly, those deep breaths," Shiori had said, "maybe you're breathing in the darkness they have inside them. Sometimes I'm thinking to myself, *You mustn't go to sleep,* even as I'm dozing off, having some terrible dream."

Shiori, it's really true, isn't it? I think lately I've started to understand. I think maybe as I'm sleeping next to him, stretched out here like his shadow, maybe I take in his very being, his heart and mind, just like breathing in the darkness. And maybe if you keep on doing that, if you come to know lots of different people's dreams, like you did, maybe you reach a point from which you can't return, and maybe that weighed down on you so heavily that in the end there was really nothing you could do but die.

No doubt it was because I was thinking about all this immediately before I tossed myself into sleep—charged in the way I always do—that I dreamed of Shiori that night, for the first time since she'd died. I could see her perfectly clearly. Everything in the dream seemed absolutely real, it was all as vivid as the world before my eyes.

I awake with a start in my room.

It's night. I can see Shiori sitting at the round wooden table in the next room, a combined kitchen and dining room, arranging flowers in a vase. She has on a pink sweater that I've often seen her in, and khaki pants, and she's wearing the same slippers she always wears.

I sit up, feeling muddled. "Shiori?" I say in a voice blurred with sleep.

"You're awake?"

Shiori glances over at me, and her stern profile becomes a soft, smiling face. Dimples dot her cheeks. Seeing her, I can't help laughing.

"Hey, you know what? I was just dreaming about Mr. Iwanaga," I say. "It was an incredibly real dream—we were sleeping together. We were lying next to each other in bed, right, and we were talking about you."

"What! Who gave you permission to bring me into your dreams?" Without looking my way, Shiori grins.

"Somehow I just can't make these look any good." She's trying to put a huge bunch of white tulips in the glass vase on the table. But the flowers' heads keep twirling restlessly in all directions, refusing to come together. There are still several tulips lying on the table.

"What if you just cut the stems?" I say.

"I don't know . . . doesn't that seem kind of cruel?"

Once again the desperate battle begins. I can't stand to just sit and watch her, so I get up and walk over. Since I've only now woken up my arms and legs move sluggishly, and the air in the room feels fresh.

"Here, let me try."

I take hold of the vase, my hands brushing lightly against Shiori's white fingers. But no matter what I do, the flowers always end up spinning around to face in whatever directions they like.

"Yeah, you're right. The tops just won't stop bending."

"Hey Terako, didn't you have a slightly taller vase? I think it was black, and a bit wider than this one?"

"Oh, that's right! Get that one, bring that! I still have it!" I say. "I think it's up toward the top of the cabinet."

"I'll bring a chair."

Shiori runs into the room where I've just been sleeping and comes back carrying a chair. She has a kind of proud expression on her face, a big smile. And so without thinking I say, "You're always smiling, aren't you, Shiori?"

"Where did that come from? Besides, it only seems that way because my eyes are so narrow." Now she's standing on the chair, and I'm gazing up at her throat from below. "This one?"

I'm gazing at her hand as it opens the cabinet.

"Right, it's in that box there, the really long one." I point at the box.

"Could you take it?" she asks.

I open the long box she's handed me and take out a large round black vase. I rinse it out, wipe it with a cloth, and pour water inside. The gurgle of the water echoes powerfully through the night.

"I bet they'll stay in place now."

Shiori steps down from the chair, gasping slightly, and for a second she grins at me. I nod back at her. She's better at arranging flowers than I am, so I pass the beautifully scented white tulips over to her, one by one. Even now she's arranging them, ever so carefully. . . .

I awoke with a start.

"What?" I cried, and sprang up in bed, naked.

Shiori . . . wasn't there.

But it had been so vivid! Suddenly I'd just tumbled down into some place that wasn't the place I'd been in, and there was a man sleeping next to me. The night was dark, the room was steeped in gray. The headlights of the cars driving past under the window looked bleary.

I sat gazing at my surroundings for a moment, and felt myself zooming back toward reality. The force of that dream had been so great that my head was booming with pain, and everything my eyes settled on seemed like a lie. Only the feeling that I'd just been back with Shiori seemed real.

I understood. Finally I felt as though I really understood what it was all about. To have someone sleep next to me— that was exactly what I needed. It was perfect for people like me. If Shiori had been lying next to me, there was no doubt at all that she'd have ended up having a dream just like the one I'd had, powerful and hot. A second reality that lures the dreamer in, ever so realistically colored, seen from a realistic angle, with the same sense of presence. . . . I sat gazing down at the bedcover in a state of shock.

"Hey," he said.

It was so sudden that I shivered. Glancing around, I saw that his eyes were wide open—that he was gazing at me. A thought slid into my brain.

So here we are again, at the edge of night.

"Why'd you sit up so fast? Were you having a bad dream?"

"No. It was a good dream," I said. "A super dream. It was great. I was so happy I didn't want to wake up. God, it's awful having to come back to a place like this. It's a total fraud!"

"She must still be half asleep," my boyfriend mumbled, as if to himself, and took my hand. Just then I felt tears welling up into my eyes. A hot teardrop plopped down onto the bedcover, and he was startled, and he pulled me back down into the covers, and even though it wasn't his fault, not really, he started being extremely earnest.

"I'm sorry . . . I didn't realize how tired you were. But it's okay, I guess we can . . . well, we won't be able to meet any more this week, but maybe next week we can get some really delicious food somewhere. Will that be all right? Hey, the fireworks are next week, aren't they? Why don't we go to the river and see them? Okay?"

His skin felt hot against my ear. I could hear his heart beating.

"But it'll be so crowded!" I said, giggling.

Tears were still trickling from my eyes, but I was feeling a little brighter.

"We should be able to see at least a little as long as we're somewhere in the neighborhood, even if we don't go right down to the riverbank. I know! Why don't we go for some eel?"

"Sounds good to me."

"Do you know any good restaurants?"

"Let's see . . . is that big place right on the road any good?"

"No, they're hopeless. They serve tempura and all sorts of other things there, you know, not just eel. That's the wrong way to go about it. Hold on, isn't there a place on one of those streets around back?"

"Oh yeah, there's that shop behind the temple. Let's go there!"

"With eel it's important that you have the feeling it's just been caught, you know, and that it's being served immediately. You've got to have that."

"The consistency of the rice and the sauce are crucial too, of course. But only, I should note, when the eel is actually being served with rice."

"Right, right. It makes you feel like you're about to throw up when the rice is mushy. God, you know eel used to be a real delicacy when I was a kid. . . ."

The two of us talked on and on about eel. And then, little by little, the trickle of our words began to dry up, and before long, at almost the same time, we'd both drifted off into a tran-

quil sleep. A sleep that was deep and warm, a sleep from which
no dream would rouse us.

His wife must be in the very deepest depths of night.
    Maybe Shiori is nearby? The darkness must be so dense . . .
    Perhaps sometimes in my sleep I wander there, too?
    These thoughts drifted through my mind just before I
woke. Then the leaden clouds hanging in the sky outside the
window slipped into my eyes, and I glanced over to my side
and saw that my boyfriend was gone. Looking over at the clock,
I was surprised to see that it was one in the afternoon. I was
completely stunned—I shook my head as I climbed out of bed.
There was a letter lying on the night table.

    You sure sleep well for someone who doesn't work.
    It seems like every woman I know is fast asleep.
    I won't wake you, you're sleeping too soundly. I've
    extended the room reservation until two. Take
    your time. I'm off to work. I'll call you.

    Each individual letter was as clearly printed as if he'd been
practicing his handwriting—it was beautiful. *Is this actually how
he writes?* I thought, and found myself overwhelmed by the
illusion that what I had before me was an image of his form, a
contour more palpable than the man I'd embraced the previous
night. I kept staring at that letter for ages.

I'd been sleeping in a T-shirt, and even though it was summer my whole body was trembling with cold. The clouds lying over the open town gleamed with silver. I gazed down at the streams of cars, the fog that addled my head still refusing to disperse, and got into my clothes. Even after I had washed my face, even after I had brushed my teeth, I felt completely unawake, and felt my drowsiness spreading, seeping slowly down into the very core of my being.

I went down to the café and had lunch, but my limbs were just floating through space, my mouth and stomach and heart were all messed up, and it was so extreme it made me sad. Several times, as I sat bathed in the enchantingly pale sunlight that streamed through the window, I felt my eyes starting to close. I tried counting my way back through the hours I'd slept. But no matter how many times I counted, the total always came out to be more than ten. *Why on earth am I still so sleepy, why don't I wake up? However sleepy oversleeping leaves me, I'm usually fine after half an hour. . . .* But even these thoughts, absorbed in them as I was, seemed not to belong to me.

My head was reeling as I climbed into the taxi that took me back to my apartment. After putting a load of clothes in the wash, I sat down on the sofa and promptly started dozing off again.

It was hopeless.

At some point I noticed that my head was drooping down ever so slowly toward the back of the sofa. I sat up with a start and began leafing through a magazine, but soon noticed that I'd been reading the same place over and over again. *God, this is just like being in class in the afternoon, falling asleep staring at a textbook,* I thought, and then closed my eyes again. The cloudy sky swept into the room . . . it was like I was having some kind of attack. Even the rumble of the washing machine couldn't keep me awake. I no longer cared about anything. I slipped out of my blouse and skirt and let them drop to the floor, then climbed into my bed. The cover felt cool and comfortable, the pillow settled gently into a lusciously sleepy shape.

I'd just begun listening to my breath as it deepened and slowed when I realized that the phone was ringing. Of course it had to be my boyfriend, that was obvious. It rang on and on, like an expression of his ever patient love, but however earnestly I tried, I just couldn't open my eyes. *It's like some sort of curse,* I thought. *My mind is perfectly clear, but I can't get up.*

A certain doubt fluttered up briefly in my mind.

Maybe his wife put this curse . . . ?

It disappeared. I could tell from the way my boyfriend spoke of her that his wife wasn't the kind of person who'd do something like this. She was an extremely gentle person.

I was much too tired. My thoughts kept changing directions, heading one way and then circling back, like someone wandering around outside at dusk, no destination in mind.

No doubt I myself am the enemy.

I felt the truth of this as my consciousness faded. Sleep slid around me like silk, slowly strangling me, sucking away my life. Then . . . blackout.

Several times I heard the phone ringing in my sleep.
The calls were from him.

*T*he room was steeped in gray the next time I awoke. I held
up my hand and looked at it, and saw that its outline was vague
and dark. A thought rose weakly through my vacant mind. *It's
evening already.*

Of course the drone of the washing machine had stopped
by then, the apartment was completely still. My head ached,
my whole body was stiff, all my joints were sore. The hands
on the clock pointed to five. I was extremely hungry. *I can eat
one of the oranges in the fridge, or that pudding, I think there was
some pudding.* . . . I climbed out of bed and put on some of the
clothes that were lying scattered on the floor.

It was very, very quiet. It was so quiet it felt like I was the
only person left alive on earth. That feeling was so strange I
can't even begin to describe it. Then when I flicked on the
lights and glanced outside the window, when I saw the paper
boy putting newspapers in the mailboxes, and saw that there
were no lights on in any of the surrounding buildings, and that
the sky to the east was orange . . . suddenly I understood.

"It's—but it's five in the morning!" I cried.

My voice sounded stale. I was afraid, seriously afraid. How
many times had the hands circled the clock? What day was it?
And what month? I hurried out of my apartment and down the
stairs, feeling like I was trapped in a nightmare, then took the

newspaper out of my box and unfolded it. Relief flooded me. *It's all right—I've only slept one night.* Yet there was no denying that I'd slept for an unusually long time. I had the sense that my whole body was slightly out of tune. I felt dizzy. The dawning blue had crept into town now, the beams of the street lamps had turned transparent. The very thought of returning to my room frightened me so much that I couldn't think of what to do. *I know I'll only fall asleep again, and I'd rather wait until I'm so desperate I no longer care.* I felt like I had nowhere to go.

And so I just walked outside.

The sky was still dark, and the suffocating scent of summer hung thick in the cool air outdoors. The only people out on the street were joggers and dog walkers, people returning home after spending the night elsewhere, and the elderly. Everyone had some purpose in mind, and compared to them I must have looked like a ghost out wandering in the dawn as I plodded along, dazed, dressed in whatever clothes I happened to have grabbed.

There wasn't really anywhere I wanted to go, so I just kept on walking slowly in the direction of the local park. It was a very small place, tucked in a little cranny on a street of houses that ran behind an apartment complex. Shiori and I used to visit it a lot on early morning walks after we'd stayed up all night. There was nothing there but a bench, a sandbox, and a swing set. I sat down on the aging wooden bench and clutched my head in my hands, like someone who's lost her job. My stomach was growling, but somehow I couldn't think of how to make it stop. What on earth had happened to me? It seemed as if I'd finally reached the point where I couldn't make myself do anything, where I no longer had the will to act. I was so sleepy I couldn't even think clearly.

The air was filling with mist, and the different colored toy animals that lay in the sandbox looked smudged, as if I were seeing them through smoke. The entire park was filled with the scent of moist greenery and the fragrance of soil. I went on holding my head in my hands, struggling to keep my eyelids from dropping. I gazed at the pattern of my skirt, which was darkened by my shadow.

"Are you feeling ill?"

A woman's voice rang out just inches from my ear. I was so horribly embarrassed that for a moment I considered acting like I really did feel sick, but the thought of how much trouble it would be if she got seriously worried made me give up on that idea. So I lifted my head. The woman was sitting right beside me, staring into my face, except that she wasn't a woman, she was a girl—she looked like she was probably in high school. She was wearing jeans. And she had these really enormous, mysterious eyes. Eyes that seemed to be gazing off into some vast distance, eyes like two crystals.

"No, I'm all right. I'm just a little tired," I said.

"Your face looks pretty pale," she said, sounding concerned.

"I'm fine, really. But thanks anyway."

I smiled at the girl, and she smiled back. The greenery shook gently in the wind and a cool fragrance swept around us and then drifted off. The girl kept sitting there next to me, she wasn't moving, and since I couldn't very well stand up and walk off myself, I kept on sitting where I was, too, staring straight ahead. She had this odd sort of aura about her—this feeling of not-quite-rightness, like she didn't belong in these surroundings. Her long hair streamed down over her shoulders; she was a lovely young woman. Yet I had the impression that something about her was off. The thought crossed my mind that she might be slightly mad. All the same, I could feel myself starting to relax, ever so slowly, just from being with her, being with someone.

Shiori and I used to sit here like this, looking at the swings, I thought. *We'd stay up all night watching videos and then in the morning we'd be so filled with energy that we couldn't get to sleep, so we'd buy a can of hot tea and a few seaweed-wrapped balls of rice at a convenience store and then come here to eat. I always hated the ones with the tuna packed in the middle, but Shiori loved that kind. . . .*

"You better go to the train station right away."

The girl spoke so suddenly that I jumped. I'd been falling asleep again. I turned to look at her and was met with an extremely severe expression. Her eyebrows had come together to form a single dark shadow. And her tone of voice was completely different now, much sharper and deeper.

"What? The station?"

I didn't know what to say. *It looks like she is crazy,* I thought, and started to feel slightly afraid. She stood up, positioned herself directly in front of me, and looked straight into my eyes. Her eyes really were strange. She was staring right at me, but the look in her eyes gave the impression that she was focusing on some point way off in the distance. I was mesmerized by those eyes, charmed. I couldn't say a word.

The girl continued, "Once you're there, go to the newsstand and pick up a copy of the *Job-Hunter's Journal*. Then look through it and find yourself a job. Even if it's only for a very short period of time, just do it. You could be some kind of model or an usher at a show or something. An office job is no good because you'll fall asleep. You need some kind of work that'll keep you standing up and moving your hands and feet around. Just go do it, all right? I can't even stand to look at you. If you go on like this you'll end up getting trapped in this mode, you know, you won't be able to go back to being what you were—that's the way you look. It frightens me."

There was nothing I could do but sit quietly and listen. It's strange, but for some reason I had the feeling that this young woman was quite a lot older than me. And it was eerie how all the things she was saying hit me so hard, how her words pierced straight through to my heart. She was entirely serious, but she didn't sound like she was angry at me. How can I explain it? She was motormouthing, and she sounded a little desperate, and at the same time a bit irritated.

"But . . . why?" I muttered.

"I doubt that we'll meet again after this. We probably only ran into each other now because you've come so near to where I am," she said. "And I'm not just suggesting that you get a job, you know. That's not the point. You see, your spirit and your psyche are both so drained, you're terribly exhausted. It's not just you, there are lots and lots of people like you. But I have this feeling that I'm the reason you're so exhausted, that you're . . . it really does seem that way. I'm sorry, I'm so very sorry. You know who I am, don't you?"

She was still staring straight into my eyes when she asked this question. Her tone made it sound as if she were casting a spell.

"Why, you're . . ."

I'd actually said this. My voice sounded peculiarly loud—I opened my eyes with a start. There was no one there in front of me, nothing but the cold mist that shrouded the park, blurring the section of the world that I could see as it drifted and eddied.

Had it been a dream?

I stood up shakily and walked from the park, still not quite sure what was what. For a moment I actually considered going to the train station, but then I've never been one of these meek fools who goes along with whatever people say—actually, I tend to be rather contrary. Even supposing it had been a dream, the simple fact that I'd had such a dream was extremely irritating; and so in the end, I just went back to my apartment and went to bed.

I didn't care anymore.

* * *

*T*hings were awful when I woke up.

I was starving, my entire body ached, my throat was parched—I felt like I'd turned into a mummy. My mind was clear, which was what you'd expect, but my body felt so heavy and drained that I couldn't even make myself get out of bed. On top of everything, it was raining.

The clock said it was noon, but even so the room was sunk in darkness, flooded with the thick rush of the falling rain. I didn't feel like putting on any music, so I just kept lying there listening to the rain, and before too long I found myself thinking of Shiori in that silent room of hers. Shiori unable to fall asleep anywhere that was soft and comfortable, swinging in that hammock, asleep.

An unbearable sadness had just started to wind itself around me when the phone rang. I knew it wasn't my boyfriend, but I figured that since I was up I might as well answer it anyway. And so I did.

*I*t was a friend of mine from college. She was calling to ask if I'd be interested in doing a little work. The company she worked for was having a trade show the following week, would I like to be a hostess? All kinds of people were always calling me up with offers like this.

I was on the verge of declining the offer—the refusal had made it as far as the base of my throat—when for some reason I blurted out, "Sure." Maybe I'd been scared by the coincidence of her calling so soon after the incident in the park, I don't know. I regretted having agreed as soon as I spoke, regretted it ferociously, but there was nothing I could do. My friend was delighted, and she'd already started rattling on, telling me where she thought we should meet and what sort of work I'd be doing. I gave up whatever hope I'd had of resisting and started jotting down what she said.

I was still just as sleepy as I'd been before.

Get up early in the morning, get myself ready, leave the apartment. It should have been perfectly simple, but I'd been holed up inside for so long just waiting for the telephone to ring that it was actually extremely grueling. There were only three days of training and then three days of actual work, but it was so hard I could barely stand it. I felt sleepy no matter what I was doing, so sleepy that I always felt like I was on the verge of disintegrating. I was mixed in with a bunch of other young women my age, and I had to remember all kinds of things at once; I had to memorize the blurbs explaining the products, and I spent the whole time on my feet—and every bit of this weighed down on me so much that it felt like a bad dream. I didn't even have time to think. Yes, I regretted agreeing to do that work more than I can say.

But even in that very brief period of time I was made abundantly aware of the extent to which various things inside

BANANA YOSHIMOTO

me had degenerated without my even knowing it. I'd always hated working, and I'd never cared much about the kinds of jobs I took or whether I had one or not or anything like that, and none of that had changed at all, it wasn't that . . . it was something like guts, the ability to move on to the next thing when I had to, it was something like hope, like anticipation. . . . I can't explain it very well. But I feel sure that this something I'd unknowingly cast aside was the same thing that Shiori had lost, was what she'd cast aside herself, also without noticing. Maybe if she'd been lucky she could have gone on living anyway, just as she was. But she was too weak, she couldn't endure a life like that. The flow was so strong that it swallowed her whole.

I'm not saying that I'd gotten a handle on my life or anything. It's just that there was something much more lively about forcing myself to get up at seven every morning, and then dashing out of my apartment and bullying my tired heart and mind and body all day, than there was in the pain I felt when I stayed cooped up in my apartment, bathed in sleep. I was so worn out that I couldn't even talk, and only managed to keep up my end of the conversation about once every three times my boyfriend called, yet the extent of my exhaustion was such that even this didn't concern me. The thought that when these six days were over I might go back to being nothing but a sleeping woman scared me so much that everything would go black. I did my best not to think about it. There were even times when I wouldn't think about my boyfriend, not at all. It was pretty unbelievable. Then, as time passed, I began to sense that the

166

sleepiness I'd felt—sleepiness so fierce it was almost amusing—was gradually, ever so gradually, draining from my body. My feet were swollen, my room got all messy, dark pockets formed under my eyes. I didn't particularly want the money, the work was pointless, and so it was extremely difficult.

The strange dream I'd had at daybreak that morning in the park was the one thing that kept me going through all this. Each morning at seven o'clock my alarm would go off and my stereo would switch on and I'd lie there in the midst of all that noise thinking what a pain everything was, and how I was so tired I could die, and that I might as well give up now . . . and then my thoughts would wander back to that daybreak, and I'd get this vague feeling that I was betraying that girl, and then I felt like I just couldn't give up. For someone as cowardly and as lazy as I am, I think I did a pretty good job of hanging in there. But those eyes, those ever so distant, sorrow-filled eyes . . . however hard I tried, I just couldn't forget them.

Come to think of it, I met my boyfriend on the job.

The place was this sort of office, really big, that designed things. It took up an enormous amount of space in this huge building, a whole floor, and there were all sorts of different sections. I didn't know much about what they were doing or how they were doing it or anything—basically my job was to answer the phone and type out stuff and punch data into the computer and make copies and deliver messages and so on. I think there were probably more than ten of us doing the same kind of work.

I'd been hired as a replacement for a cousin of mine who'd gone to stay with a family in the United States, so I was only there for three months, but even so I did my best to give people the impression that I was a bit of a fool. It's not that I'm particularly clever or anything, but I know that if you work too hard in a place like that, your workload just gets heavier and heavier and you end up losing a lot more than you gain. So I elected not to do very much. There's nothing as senseless as being harried at a simple do-what's-needed part-time job. So I worked in a sort of haze the whole time, keeping only about one third of my circuits open. As a result I'd show up late and make mistakes, enter data into the wrong columns, send out perfectly blank faxes, that kind of thing, and even though none of this was on purpose I still ended up doing each of these things about once every three days, so that soon people stopped asking me to do anything at all difficult and my work got a whole lot easier.

It happened one Sunday. The company had a vacation, but I'd gone in on my own to fix a mistake I'd made the day before. I was all alone in the spacious, silent office. I was typing in some data, taking my time, when all of a sudden I started feeling inexplicably uneasy.

I had this sense that at some point during my two months of acting the fool I'd actually become one—that it might not be possible for me to work any faster. It was a stupid thing to get worked up about, but at the time it seemed very serious. The longer I stared at the computer's green screen the more I worried. *I'd thought I was only keeping my talents hidden, but in fact office work is probably one of those things that I just can't do.* I struggled to keep myself from thinking about it, but I couldn't. And then—conscious all the while of how idiotic I was being— I found myself being lured on by an irresistible temptation to see what I could do. I'd seen that there was no one else in the office. And so the race began. Thinking back on that day now, I can see that I was still awfully young then. I started typing in all the data I had in front of me with a truly incredible vigor. For the first time in ages I relished the sensation of having my hands move with speed and accuracy, of knowing that I could do this if I tried, and I felt wonderfully contented. Before long I'd finished the corrections I'd been working on, and so—riding the crest of my energy—I decided to prepare a few of the forms that had started piling up. I began typing things into the word processor, humming as I worked. I felt like someone who'd just been granted permission to use her right hand again after being forced for ages and ages to use only her left. I guess a sort of stress must have been building up inside me all along, because I was truly thrilled with the gorgeous pages of text that emerged from the printer. Photocopying requires almost no time at all when you take it seriously. I lost myself in the work and ended up doing all kinds of little tasks that were meant to be done by others.

After about two hours of work I'd finished everything, so I heaved a heavy sigh and stood up from my desk—and then

I saw him. He was sitting quietly at a desk all the way in the very back of the empty, bright room. It was a terrible shock. I hadn't noticed him at all. He wasn't my boss or anything like that, but he worked in a section that I helped out in fairly often. He certainly knew how utterly useless I'd been as a worker. *Damn*, I thought. It looked as if he'd been waiting to see when I'd notice him, looking forward to that moment with a good deal of pleasure. He was grinning.

"Have you been here all along, then?" I said.

"Obviously you can work if you try . . . and yet somehow I don't even feel like pointing that out," he said.

And then he was laughing so hard he almost fell off his chair.

*W*e went to get some tea after that. The café we chose was a small one across from our building. It was near twilight already, and there were a few other couples besides us in the shop, having some fun on their day off. Everyone was speaking very quietly, almost whispering.

"You know, earlier, it was like watching you with the film speeded up. Why don't you always work like that?" he asked.

I considered various answers, trying to come up with something witty, but in the end all I could say was, "It's just a temp job."

"That makes sense," he said, and chuckled again for a few moments. I was continually surprised at how pure his deep voice sounded when he was talking as a regular person rather than a coworker, and by the perfect coordination of his gestures. I'd never looked at him with much attention before. I'd noticed the ring that he wore on his left hand by then. But we drank our tea without talking about any of that stuff. To tell the truth I was terribly disappointed to see that he was married.

Once, as he was recrossing his legs, he bumped one of the saucers on the table and made a clatter. He was more apologetic than he needed to be. He kept saying, "I'm sorry, I'm so sorry."

I really fall for that kind of thing, for good manners. I have this feeling that people like that never do anything truly awful to anyone else. But then on the other hand, you might say that I fall for people who can do awful things and get away with it.

We weren't particularly nervous, but still we didn't talk much. He was extremely decorous, and his profile made a very peculiar impression on me, and every so often he'd start telling me about this or that or something else. I just nodded and listened. And as I nodded I had this vague sort of intuition that he was going to be someone who'd take on a great significance in my life. It was evening and yet it seemed like morning— maybe that's why I felt this way. It was as if we were sitting around some table still half asleep, hardly speaking, that's the kind of scene it was. I imagined all kinds of warm, pleasant things that might happen between us in the future, but for some reason everything ended up turning into an image of winter. A white room filled with steam, the two of us walking along wearing coats, a wintry grove of trees. Everything I saw was like that. And this made me terribly sad.

Somehow or other that seemingly eternal week passed. I arrived back at my apartment after the last day of work and took off my clothes, just letting them lie where they fell, then chucked the envelope that held my salary on the floor and stood there giggling. And then the phone rang.

"Hey. It's me, Mr. Iwanaga," he said.

I felt a kind of nostalgia when I heard his voice.

"I haven't heard from you in a while," I said.

"Were you asleep?"

"Nope. As a matter of fact I was just standing here looking down at the envelope with my salary in it and laughing. I'm so exhausted!"

"You mean you've been working? You really are odd."

"Helps to pass the time," I said.

It occurred to me that after I'd picked up the clothes that were scattered around the room I would just go ahead and sleep as long as I liked. My head was clear, my body was completely worn out. This time it wouldn't frighten me a bit even if I slept for an entire day.

"You sure sound lively. Like when we first met."

His voice was bright. Even he'd gotten caught up in the mood.

"Now that you mention it, it's true, isn't it?" I said, scraping little flakes of worn-out nail polish off my fingernails. "By the way . . . your wife was in high school when you met her, wasn't she? And she had long hair?"

"How'd you know? Did you learn to read minds at your job or something?" He sounded suspicious. "But you're right. She was eighteen."

"I thought so," I said.

Suddenly my eyes filled with tears. Even I didn't really understand why I was crying. "Anyway . . ." he said. Then he started telling me where we should meet for that eel dinner we'd planned, and for the fireworks. As I listened to his voice and scribbled out a note to myself, my hand and the whole room and everything in it became a hot blur, vaguely bright, shining.

*T*he broad avenue that led down to the riverbank was already closed to traffic. People had spread out until they filled the entire street, and they were walking on toward the river, the fireworks. Everyone was dressed in light cotton kimonos, and they were carrying their kids up on their shoulders, and they were glancing up at the sky, laughing and making noise, and the crowd streamed on like it does at the huge Gion Festival in Kyoto, everyone moving in the same direction. I'd never seen anything like it. I felt a sort of excitement—a great rush. No one had any idea when the fireworks would finally unwind across the sky we were all watching, so we were all filled with expectation. Every face I saw was bright and cheerful.

"There's no way we'll make it to the river. Look at the crowds."

My boyfriend sounded disappointed. I looked up at his sweaty face.

"That's okay. We'll be able to see at least a little, right?" I said.

"Maybe not. We'd have to be somewhere high up."

"Well, it doesn't matter. As long as we can hear them."

If I stood on tiptoe I could see that ahead of us there was a line of people waiting to cross the bridge, and that around the end of the line a massive crowd had gathered. The night sky was bathed in deep indigo, and it was incredibly wide. Police officers stood here and there in the dark. People pressed on as if they were being channeled along by ropes. But my boyfriend and I stopped before we'd even reached the end of the line.

What was important wasn't the fireworks, it was that we were together this evening, together in this place, looking up into the sky at the same time. It was important that we link our arms and turn our faces up so that we were looking in the same direction as the people around us, and listen to the huge boomings of the fireworks. The rising energy of the crowd prodded me into a state of jittery excitement. At some point along the way my boyfriend had started wanting to see the display, too, really wanting to see it, and looking up at his face

I could tell that he could hardly wait for it to start, and somehow it seemed like he'd become young again.

I think that at some point along the way the feeling of being healthy must have come back to me. Even if all this has been nothing but the story of a few small waves that shook me when I lost my friend and wore myself out doing all the little things one does every day, even if all this was nothing but the story of a small resurrection, it still makes me think that people are very strong. I can't remember anymore whether this kind of thing ever happened to me back in the old days, but I know that when I turned to confront the darkness inside me, when somewhere way down deep inside I was really hurting, when I was utterly exhausted, all of a sudden a totally unexpected and inexplicable strength came gushing up within me.

Nothing has changed in me and nothing has changed between us. Yet all along I felt positive that I wanted to go on being with him, wanted to keep being shaken by those little waves. I've made my way through the worst of it now. I'm not too clear on what that "worst" was, but that's how I feel. With things as they are now, I might even be able to start liking someone else.

But I didn't think I would. No, I just wanted to recapture the incredibly vivid love we'd had at first—the love I'd shared with the tall man standing next to me, with the man I adored. I wanted to hold everything in place with my thin little arm and my weak spirit. I wanted to do what I could with my unreliable body to try and deal with all the many scary things that were going to start happening to us from now on. I wanted to try.

I felt like I'd just woken up a moment ago, and everything looked so clear and beautiful it was frightening. Everything really was gorgeous. Those crowds of people walking through the night, the light from the paper lanterns dotting the arcade, the line of my boyfriend's forehead as he gazed straight up, eager for the fireworks to start, as we stood there in the slightly cool wind—it was all so beautiful.

Suddenly everything seemed too perfect, and tears welled up in my eyes. Everything my gaze encountered as I looked around at the scene before us felt precious to me, and I was happy that when I'd finally woken up it had been now and here. This street was usually filled with cars, but now it had turned into a vast wide-open space, and we were standing in the middle, waiting to see the fireworks, and later we'd go and have our eel dinner, and then fall asleep, lying side by side. . . . It occurred to me how splendid it was to be able to look around at this night—this night, when we could do all these things—with a mind and a spirit so marvelously clear.

I felt almost like I was praying.

May every sleep in this world be equally peaceful.

Finally a huge boom tumbled through the sky, and over to one side of an enormous building half a ring of fireworks flickered into view, tinting the blackness for just an instant with all its colors, like a design seen through lace.

"Wow! Did you see that? I could only see a little, but . . ."

He spoke out of sympathy for me, because I'm short, but at the same time he was as thrilled as a child. He gave my shoulder a little shake.

"Yes, I could see it. It was so small it was kind of cute, wasn't it? Like a doily or something," I said.

The little clusters of light that sprayed up suddenly into the clear night sky seemed to be so far off you could hardly believe they were fireworks.

"It's true. They look like miniature fireworks."

My boyfriend was still looking up at the sky as he replied. One after the other the fireworks streamed into the night, cheers rose from the crowds, and then a moment later a giant boom would reel by overhead. People were still flowing noisily on in the direction of the riverbank, and the crowds were growing thicker, they kept moving on past us, around us . . . but he and I just kept on standing where we were, gazing up into the night sky. We felt a strange fondness for the tiny bursts of fire that we glimpsed from time to time off to the side of the skyscraper, and we kept our arms locked tightly together as we stood there, fantastically excited, waiting for the next round of fireworks to explode.

faber and faber

A Fine Balance
Rohinton Mistry

Winner of the 1996 Commonwealth Writers Prize
Shortlisted for the 1996 Booker Prize

Set in mid-1970s India, **A Fine Balance** is a subtle and com-
pelling narrative about four unlikely characters who come
together in circumstances no one could have foreseen soon
after the government declares a 'State of Internal
Emergency'. It is a breathtaking achievement: panoramic
yet humane, intensely political yet rich with local detail; and
above all, compulsively readable.

'This is a work of genius. I cannot begin to review it without
saying so. It should be read by everyone who loves books,
win every prize, make its author a millionaire. **A Fine
Balance** is *the* India novel, the novel readers have been
waiting for ever since E. M. Forster and J. G. Farrell.'
Literary Review

faber and faber

The Buddha of Suburbia
Hanif Kureishi

Winner of the Whitbread First Novel Award

'Fizzing with energy, bubbling with warmth, salty, satirical and very, very funny.' *Daily Mail*

'A first novel to cherish because it is so splendidly itself.' *Financial Times*

'Funny, perceptive and moving, it should be read by anyone who enjoys the very best of contemporary writing.' *Evening Standard*

'One of the best comic novels of growing up, and one of the sharpest satires on race relations in this country that I've ever read.' *Independent on Sunday*

'It is a wonderful novel. I doubt I will read a funnier or one with more heart, this year, possibly this decade.' Angela Carter, *Guardian*

'This is exactly the novel one hoped Hanif Kureishi would write: utterly irreverent and wildly improper, but also genuinely touching and truthful. And very funny indeed.' Salman Rushdie

faber and faber

Red Earth and Pouring Rain
Vikram Chandra

'Chandra is imagining and writing with such originality and intensity as to be not merely drawing on myth but making it.' *Sunday Times*

'Makes its British counterparts look like apologetic throat-clearings.' Adam Thorpe

faber and faber

The Remains of the Day
Kazuo Ishiguro

Winner of the Booker Prize

In the summer of 1956, Stevens, the ageing butler of Darlington Hall, embarks upon a leisurely motoring holiday that will take him deep into the English countryside and into his past . . .

A haunting tale of lost causes and a lost love, **The Remains of the Day** contains Ishiguro's now celebrated evocation of life between the wars in a Great English House – within those walls can be heard ever more distinct echoes of the violent upheavals spreading across Europe.

'A remarkable, strange and moving book.' *Independent*

'**The Remains of the Day** is a triumph . . . This wholly convincing portrait of a human life unweaving before your eyes is inventive and absorbing, by turns funny, absurd, and ultimately very moving.' *Sunday Times*

'**The Remains of the Day** is a dream of a book: a beguiling comedy of manners that evolves almost magically into a profound and heart-rending study of personality, class and culture.' *New York Times Book Review*

faber and faber

Amongst Women
John McGahern

Winner of the Irish Times–Aer Lingus Irish Literature Prize
for Fiction 1990
Shortlisted for the Booker Prize 1990

Moran is an old Republican whose life was transformed for
ever by his days of glory as a guerrilla leader in the War of
Independence. Now, in old age, living out in the country,
Moran is still fighting – with his family, his friends, even
himself – in a poignant struggle to come to terms with the
past.

'A masterpiece.' John Banville

'Though it bears no trace of strain, no whiff of midnight
oil, it is obviously the product of much loving labour. It is
compact but not dense, spare yet rich, and brimming with
tension.' *Observer*

Please send me

	title	ISBN	Price
_____	The New York Trilogy *Paul Auster*	15223 6	£6.99
_____	Jack Maggs *Peter Carey*	19377 3	£6.99
_____	Oscar and Lucinda *Peter Carey*	15304 6	£7.99
_____	Red Earth and Pouring Rain		
_____	*Vikram Chandra*	17456 6	£7.99
_____	Pig Tales *Marie Darrieussecq*	19372 2	£6.99
_____	Hullabaloo in the Guava Orchard		
_____	*Kiran Desai*	19571 7	£6.99
_____	The Last King of Scotland *Giles Foden*	19564 4	£6.99
_____	Headlong *Michael Frayn*	20147 4	£6.99
_____	Lord of the Flies *William Golding*	19147 9	£6.99
_____	The Remains of the Day *Kazuo Ishiguro*	15491 3	£6.99
_____	The Unconsoled *Kazuo Ishiguro*	17754 9	£7.99
_____	The Poisonwood Bible *Barbara Kingsolver*	20175 X	£7.99
_____	Immortality *Milan Kundera*	14456 X	£7.99
_____	The Unbearable Lightness of Being		
_____	*Milan Kundera*	13539 0	£6.99
_____	The Buddha of Suburbia *Hanif Kureishi*	14274 5	£6.99
_____	Aunt Julia and the Scriptwriter		
_____	*Mario Vargas Llosa*	16777 2	£7.99
_____	Amongst Women *John McGahern*	16160 X	£6.99
_____	A Fine Balance *Rohinton Mistry*	17936 3	£7.99
_____	Birds of America *Lorrie Moore*	19727 2	£6.99
_____	Our Fathers *Andrew O'Hagan*	20106 7	£6.99
_____	The Bell Jar *Sylvia Plath*	08178 9	£6.99

**To order these titles phone Bookpost on 01624 836000
Or complete the order form below:**

I enclose a cheque for £ _____ made payable to Bookpost PLC
Please charge my: o Mastercard   o Visa   o Amex   o Delta
o Switch   Switch Issue No_____

Credit Card No	Expiry date
Name	
Address	
	Postcode
Signed	Date

Free postage and packing in the UK.
Overseas customers allow £1 per pbk/ £3 per hbk.
Send to: Bookpost PLC, PO Box 29, Douglas, Isle of Man, IM99 1BQ
fax: 01624 837033 email: bookshop@enterprise.net
http://www.bookpost.co.uk